A TRADE

Harriso

CU00329735

ALSO BY HARRISON ABBOTT

NOVELS

Amazed Gloom

Filippo's Game

Polly's Dreams

Magpie Glen

Fox and the Birch Trees

Tannahills

SHORT STORIES

One Hundred Ticks

PART ONE

MARVIN

A dog barks. Somewhere off in the street, shrill and stupid and short and then it stops and Marvin hangs back for a period, to make sure that nobody appears. He hasn't heard any such noise in hours and he's been walking all night and now it's a late-September early morning, just on the cusp of dawn. Windy and with an odd whiteness in the sky with sparky showers. Marvin watches the leaves on the roadsides meddle and bustle and he remembers being a kid kicking them about. But now the mass foliage has yet to fall and though the trees are tired they're not overly bare: it's been a warm month and the cold hasn't really arrived yet. ...

There's still a sense of unease. About that dog. It came too close and Marvin begins to feel wide open out on the concrete and something tells him to step off the road and into this park, which is just by it; he crosses and gets to a wall which he climbs over and he jumps into the weeds by the other side. Nettles. Bramble bushes and there are a few blackberries, very few, still dotted around them and these are a quizzical score but Marvin must stay quiet for now and wait and hide. He presses his back against the wall. ... Nearby, too, there's a handsome elderberry tree and there is this fat woodpigeon munching away at those berries. Despite her weight she perches quite effortlessly on the leaves and just kinda floats there pecking them up and is quite content ... until there's another dog bark from down the street. Marvin flinches. The woodpigeon up and flies away. Marvin has his weapon. He's also never used it and he finds himself trembling and idiotic. Not built for this type of ordeal. He waits. What kind of dog is it? What if the dog smells him and comes over? ... Then it gets worse. Because he hears voices. People out there behind him. In bobbles of sound. And they louden and near. Male, plural. It's hard to tell the tone of their voices. Marvin guesses they're around the same age as he is (Marvin's 29 and he estimates they must be late twenties/early thirties also). ... The wall really isn't that tall and his head hangs only a yard from the top and Marvin feels the strength of the air over him. Then there are words. They're speaking in an eerily conversational way. As if everything in the city is okay. ... Then the dog growls. Marvin hears a pitter-patter of paws and then the growling intensifies, right behind his back, just through the wall. He reaches into his inside jacket pocket and holds the handle of his handgun, this implement which he's fired a few times but which he's never yet *used* and his grasp is all twitchy and the veins in his wrist pump and pump. ... His fear was a prudent one: the dog's smelled him and knows that he's there. The men have gone silent. Until one of them shouts a name – a common girl's name – and then yells, "Come on, now." And the growls cease and the paws skitter away and Marvin suspends there in the awkward crouch and the men's voices continue up and up the road and away from him. He eases the handgun back in his pocket. Waits several minutes. And then slowly knees up and peers over the edge of the wall. In the far distance there are three dots of men almost disappearing at the summit of the street and then they go and he can't see the dog. Phew. Marvin relaxes a tad. He moves out of the weeds and sits down on the grass and the trees whoosh around him. From his bag he takes his bottle of water and drinks from it. ... The woodpigeon makes a comeback. As in, it just puffs into vision again, returning to the elderberries where it commences eating. Marvin smiles: wishes he could be a pigeon, in a way. He gets up. Must move on.

Goes through the park. At length he finds that one of the bins has been knocked over. By something, and its contents are spewed across the grass and Marvin finds it a shame. Juice cartons, bottles, crisp packets, corporate logos. All their colours seem to him a bit surreal, incongruous. There's a banana skin there too. It's totally blackened and crisp as if it's been burnt ... He reaches the end of the park where there are gates. Which are actually locked. He scales the gates, clumsily and drops off back onto the road. Marvin scouts about, to spot any movements, and there's nothing and he goes on and this street eventually opens out into a broader one, one which would've been heavy with traffic if time were reversed by four weeks. A month back there would be vehicles rolling by even if it were this early in the morning. Now it's deserted. A long stretch. Marvin again gets nervous because he is small and exposed in this environment. So he quickens his step. The wind rushes his hair and eyes and the general temperature is an exact mix of hot/cold. He comes across a bus stop. Its windowpanes have been smashed apart and the glass lies in impressive glittery rubble across the floor and Marvin kinda enjoys the way the shards sound under his boots and his soles are more than thick enough to bear them. ... Looks like they just bashed it up for fun. A small while later he finds a solitary shoe – a red stripey trainer – lying marooned on its backside. Then he comes upon the tram tracks and their cable lines are sad and confused in the air, and he takes this as a cue to take a narrower street because these tracks lead into the meatier part of the city ... He successfully finds a shorter route. With office buildings arising either side of him. And it's strange to walk through them. With all of their windows looking down at him; hundreds of eyes and zilch lights on, zilch people in them: mass grey drawings awaiting demolition. Marvin can't quite feel right anywhere he goes and this is probably a wise thing, despite the constant sweating and the ticks of the head and that sharpness in the tonsils and the way he can barely eat and yet doesn't get hungry. He needs to get out of the city. Must keep trying.

ELISA

Will anybody still be there? Elisa heard them the other night, crashing and hooting. In this flat. Which isn't hers, where she never lived in before. Which, when she found it, had its front door open and she'd sneaked in to avoid what was happing outside. Elisa's been here for perhaps forty hours and it's very early morning now. (About the same time that Marvin is walking in that park. Albeit Marvin wanders in another part of the city, and Elisa and he have never met each other.) Yesterday Elisa ate the last of the apples of the bag she had and she'd had no food throughout the night and she was too scared of the dark to go out and nor could she sleep and so she sat on this anonymous sofa in a room with almost nothing to do but scribble in her diary. ... Now, in this morning, she writes on a new page, "I'm heading out now. I won't be coming back here," and she dates it and puts it in her bag. And leaves. She goes to the end of the corridor and through a FIRE door and into a new stairwell where her shoes make spidery echoes throughout the arena. Louder is the volume of hollow whirling wind which she presumes correctly to come through the front doors at the bottom of the staircase, and she ventures through them and it's profound and dazzling to be outside again. Elisa lifts her hood up. ... Elisa is eight years old. She has light brown hair and is naturally very thin. When she heard the mayhem two nights back she thought that they would come down the street and into the flat and find her and kill her gorily and as she lay quivering in the gloom she wondered what heaven would be like and somehow there didn't seem any possibility of a 'heaven', even though she'd always believed in something like that beforehand, despite never having quite pondered death up to this point. ... So, she's on her way to the supermarket. Because she saw that in the *daylight* a couple days back and is hoping that there might be some food in there, if indeed the looters didn't take every single item. Elisa's already looted herself. Several times. Because she's had to. ... The supermarket's a chubby construction. Like a disgruntled cube. Elisa gets to the edge of the car park and she pauses and scans the area. There are trolleys upended and plumed about across the giant outlined pitch ... Umm, and a black mark of another object which she can't make out from this distance. Until she goes closer and it's a bicycle. An indigo bike. It lies at a skewed angle and the front tyre is bent. And beside it on the cement is a purpling splodge and splash, which changes Elisa's breath and the splotches of them lead away in a trail, red purple stains. She winces away from it. The scene, and picks her way through the trolleys and comes eventually to the supermarket entrance. Looks within. To a dusty uncertain space which she's unsure of entering. She's come all this way now so why turn back. Onwards.

The oxygen is pumped with dust as well and she goes in too confidently and gets a great whack of it in the mouth and spends her initial seconds coughing. And is afraid of the noise she makes. Because there might be others here. … She wipes her eyes with the tissue from her pocket which is already too old and mucky. The newspaper stall is close by. It's entirely untouched by the rioting. Out of curiosity she goes over to the stalls just to see what they're like. Honestly, there are about a hundred newspapers here and none of them are scathed. The date on all of them is 30th August, so that was 27 days back exactly. And the headlines have similar jargon, no matter their political wing or journalistic class; STOCK MARKET CHAOS, BANKS IN TURMOIL, 'CRASH' 'CRASH' 'CRASH', DISASTER, CREDIT TUMBLES, MARKETS PLUNGE, BIGGEST FALL … 'FEARS TRIGGER PANIC SELLING' … One of the tabloids has the ugly cheek to purport the pun, 'SHOCK MARKET'. … Elisa picks up a newspaper. (Not that tabloid one but another of them.) Because she just thinks it might be useful one day – a kind of historical document, perhaps – and puts it in her bag. … Beside the newspaper bit is the snacks/candy bit, which is comatose, deserted. She continues by what used to be the vegetable and fruit crates and by the meat and cheese aisle. The other aisle leading on from that is the gardening one and she can see bags of compost and nice pots and flower seeds barbecue shit and whatnot. None of it is of any use. … The rice and pasta sections are spent. They even cleared out the vegan section and the wacky canned vegetables nobody usually seems to go for unless they're in big meals, umm, and she's beginning to lose hope when she's turning into the next lane. Which has a SOUP banner above it. She slips along studying the shelves and then she finds a jumble of blobs within the murk. Items! At the very back of the shelf, bottom shelf, and she reaches ahead and clasps one of them and brings it out. It's a can of soup. What a peal of luck! Lentil soup. The ones with the 'low salt' blue labels. There are two more of them as well so that's three cans, she now has, of food. And she doesn't see why she should wait. So she opens one. And the smell of the vegetables strikes her nose. She has no cutlery or bowl and the soup will be cold but none of these things matter and she drinks from the edge of the can and the contents froth in her mouth and this exhilaration goes through her. ... It's all berserk. And because her stomach is so intolerant, it smarts at the food. She drinks/eats fast. And her stomach rebels and she thinks she might throw up. This won't be good. So she calms herself and rests and orders herself not to vomit. *Just be easy. Ease down. You're not going to be sick. You've got food now. You're not going to starve.* And her efforts work, because her abdomen softens and stops shuddering. Elisa sits. Children think differently and perceive the universe with an alternate zeal; the misfortune in their naivety is that the don't think to appreciate it while they can: they don't realise that they're in the zone of childhood, they simply experience it.

BANG.

There's a bang inside this supermarket and it floods Elisa with terror. She puts the can on the floor softly. And listens. Where did it come from? Ominous seconds of silence lug on, and on. She stands up. Blood reaches her head. She can't remember exactly where she is in the supermarket and how far she is from the entrance, at least not off the top of her head. Unzipping her bag, she places the two other cans of soup in, zips it back up and then walks down the aisle – back the way she came. And gets to the verge of it and peers around the corner ... into the main aisle, where at that end of it is a twitching shape of a man, standing oddly still in the middle of the hall. Elisa gulps. And retreats and goes off and tries to walk fast without her shoes making noise. Thus she heads farther into the store. One of the baskets which used to hold the bread baguettes is knocked over and she has to avoid it and after that there are all these other trays muddled about and she steps between them and her feet feel awfully brittle. She's careful, and has no clue where she's going, and it's getting darker and harder to see the ground. ... Behind her there's a scuffling sound ... or is there? Is she imagining? A marble of sweat rolls off her nose and disappears. Her sentience is all amok and she makes the mistake of not looking in front of her and she bumps into something hard. Which is followed by a huge blast. She's bumped into one of the tall baskets and she can't even see all the stuff that she's knocked over. And Elisa thinks, *the hell with it: just start running.*

She sprints until she meets a dead end, dead wall. Okay so this must be the back of the building. There could be a fire exit somewhere nearby? She pants. And something catches her eyes down the lane. Torchlight. It's that man, holding a torch, and he's just arrived at that bit where she knocked over the casket. He's thirty yards away. She squeaks. And maybe the man hears her, because the torch switches up to her. And she's illuminated. She screams. And this man bellows, "Hey! You there!" Then him and the nasal nasty light chase her. ...Elisa is quite fast for an eight year old girl, she just doesn't know it. And it's often useful not to realise a talent – because it just does its job on its own. So she reaches the end of this lane pretty well and then she's in the main artery of the market and she judges that if she gets down here she'll be at the front door again and onwards she pelts and the problem with the situation is that this man is not naturally fast himself but he's an adult and male and by those few guttural words he hollered a moment ago he means no precious news. ... *He* then gets to the main alley. "Stop right there you cunt!" he yells. He gains on her. She wonders why he sees her as a target? What has she ever done to him? She knows she won't be able to outrun him. He gets so close that she hears his jowls thrashing with saliva, and the torch makes these insane shadows and flashes on the linoleum about her legs ... And then there's a *scoosh*, some obscure audio, and at the same instant, the light exits the scene. Elisa turns. He's slipped and fallen over and he's lying there swearing to himself at his own idiocy. And dropped his torch, which has spun away and lies in a corner of a stall. ... She's lucky. Take the lucky chance! She pelts to the top of the lane and comes back to that atrium bit where she refinds the newspapers and then there are the doors and daylight and she zooms out into that and the power of the sun is refreshing and realistic and she keeps her pace up the entire way across the carpark. Until her lungs can't operate anymore because her chest will explode and she stops and looks back and there is no man chasing her any longer. ...

One of the trolleys is sitting/standing upright and she goes and sits on it and rests. It's amazing how she never even caught a proper sight of that man – whoever on earth he was – as in, a definite visual descriptive sight of him. And she'll never know what he would've done if he'd caught her. And she allows her ribcage to mellow. Then she exits the carpark. Despite everything that's just happened, she has two cans of soup in her bag now. So starvation should be postponed for at least a few more days yet.

Elisa reaches a big road with a quartet of traffic alleys across it and it's enticing to walk across them as a lone human and she imagines somebody taking a photograph of her from afar. Her body. With the blue coat and the small greasy crop of brown hair, frazzly in the wind. She proceeds for a steady while and these plains get sparser and it's optimistic to know that she's closer to the outskirts of the city. Only that nothing is definite yet. The motorway leads onto a river. Or rather, passes over this modest river and there's a bridge and she stops and looks down at the water and she likes it. So she crosses to the other side. And then steps over the fence and into the undergrowth and picks her way down the grass all the way to the bankside. The water has a soothing quality. It's not safe to drink. But there's a calmness to the trickling and sluicing and she heads along the bank until she's under the bridge and finds a place to sit down. And she would *like* to eat another can of the soup. But knows that she must keep it rationed. … However, she still has her diary. So she brings that out. Underneath the bridge there is a lofty sense of forgottenness, a sleepy shading, an underrated metal canopy right above her. And the wind makes these fantastical loops and whoops through the architecture and she could be anywhere in the world. In her diary she scribes. She writes about what happened with the man in the supermarket. … When somebody writes in a diary there is never much objective reason for it; it's impossible to tell whether anybody else cares about your thoughts: though to chronicle your days does seem medicinal.

You make a book that nobody will likely ever read, and yet it's still important. It levels your hectic mind.

ANTHONY BURTON

Anthony Burton fears he'll miss his place. If indeed he'll never be able to return. He's attached further locks to the door, the last few days, in the hope that they won't be able to kick it open. There's a sick fury in all this. Over what's happened to the city, nation, to the State: he'd expected something like this might erupt. He'd planned to retire in this apartment and has lived in it for fifteen years. Outside in the street his van waits. Wherein he's packed his most precious items. Things he can't leave behind. But of course there are many things he can't fit in which he'll have to leave, for now. *The winter will kill off the rioting*, he wishes. *The cold extinguishes armies, mass movements. Then I can come back, maybe in January. And the place could be left untouched, and I'll move back in and will relax. ...* Anthony moves his final box out and makes a final wish for the flat, and he puts the box down and locks all four locks with his keys and then heads down the corridor. Many of his neighbours have already bailed. Down the stairs and outside. It is night and the streetlamps blaze against it in shrill silver plots. He puts the box in the back of the van and shuts the doors. It really is heavily loaded, the vehicle, and he has this regressive worry that the whole thing might collapse and the wheels buckle under him as he's driving. Will just have to wait and see. ... Anthony gets in the front seat and it's chilly inside. He has a snowy beard, and hair, and yet his eyebrows have never lost their jetblack for some reason. Fancies a smoke before he sets off. And enjoys a pipe – just the way he does smoking, so be it if it's old fashioned. He undoes the window and puffs out of it. Makes a few rings. Nicotine zap kinda cheers him up. Gives him a bit of bravery. When he's finished he chucks the pipebowl embers out of the window and then shuts that and then ignites the van and then he leaves. ... And that smoking cheer-up was fleeting because as he goes/departs/evacuates, a terrific sadness envelops him, and a type of uncertain dread, considering he's never had to do anything like this before. And he's essentially improvising. ... But it's done now. He will just have to deal with it. ... ... Within his district he sees no person or vehicle or anything animate at all and he exits speedily. And yet he must turn the other direction, on the way to the bridge, because he knows that within the shorter route (on those particular roads) there was trouble a few nights back. The land rises. He goes through a suburb.

Where there are bungalows painted in rainbows and he already knows most of them have been ransacked and so he chooses not to look at them. On he continues to the next district where the housing is different but the roads are broad and he just concentrates on the driving. At one moment, another vehicle appears. Suddenly. A firework ripping down the other side. It's scary to him. Even though it's just a car and the whole passing of either vehicle lasts ten seconds and then it ploughs on away after him. Anthony orders himself to stop being so jittery. ... The urbanity drops away. Replaced by trees and fields and not-quite-countryside-just-yet because we're nearing the sea now and the bridge. (Anthony's been looking up the bridge for days, just to see whether it will appear in the news. In case anything's happened to it. He hasn't seen anything.) And, yes, when he gets there there seems nothing damaged or dodgy about it; it's cable-stayed and he gets onto it and through the poles he can see down onto the sea's expanse below and the water is quite indifferent and mammoth and planetary. (Again, here, Anthony's imagination takes a little detour and he imagines driving his van off into the abyss and wondering how long it would take to hit the surface and how far he would sink thereafter.) He finishes the bridge and there are further jaunty fields. Despite the hint of country, Anthony is nowhere near out of the city limits ... His best friend lives up north. And has offered to help him out. To shelter him. It will take days to get there and at least another day to be rid of the city zone. ... The motorway expands. Floodlights make triangles on the yellow stripes before him. And, intermittently, he goes under overpasses; those stark craning structures a-loom. ... The interior of the van has warmed up by now and he's feeling a bit more confident. He comes upon a new district, on the outskirts: he can see the lights of houses in the distance in specks of orange. Which largen as he approaches. And there are more of those overpass cranes. He's going at forty miles per hour. ... He's approaching one of these overpasses. And he thinks he sees people atop this one; figures, stickmenlike, as you would see them atop a hill in silhouette. And of course Anthony is going so fast that he doesn't have much time to hesitate or think about it. And he nears and nears the underpass and he *definitely*, now, spots people up there. ... He's *just* entering the cave of the pass. When, wham. His windscreen bursts. This colossal noise and his first reaction is to swear and then accelerate and then flume on, whilst this giant jagged mark skittles there in the glass before him. He can't see clearly beyond it. ... So he gets a way away from the overpass and then he parks the van, still wondering what's just happened. He opens his door and steps outside his vehicle. And looks back at the pass. And there are these (what look like) teenagers, girls and boys, standing there on top. Laughing and waving at him. Hahahaha hyena cackles. And then they all run off and flee. ... They lobbed something at his van. ... Anthony's more surprised than any other emotion. He's alone now on the motorway. He goes to the front of the van to inspect the damage: it's bad, a huge cragged bash as if bullets have just gone through it. ... But what *was* it? That the kids threw? He's interested to know and so he walks back to the underpass and onto the other side. ... And finds this traffic cone there. Red+fluorescentWhite with a black bottom and gloatingly lying on its side. Those young'uns hurled a traffic cone at him, just for their own entertainment ... Anthony picks it up. Because it's lying right in the middle of the road and another vehicle might hit it and it could cause a proper crash. And he throws it into the ditch and it lands with a muffled plop in the rugged grass. And because he's in such sterile territory he worries that he might get hit by an oncoming vehicle himself and so he returns to his van and gets in, and looks ahead. Right. So the smash is just left to his vision and he can still see, for the large part, in front of him. Can still drive, basically. He swears. Again. Then turns the key and steps down on the pedals.

RUBY-ROSE

Ruby-Rose is a university student in her second year. At least she was before they suspended the academic semester because of the riots; and shortly afterwards her own campus was attacked. When nobody was even inside it, and they robbed all the IT equipment and then simply hung out there drunkenly for days and moved on whence bored ... (Ruby-Rose is remarkably beautiful; she's unaware of how pretty she is. Stellar eyelashes, a short, pouting jaw and these blooming lips. She's nineteen years old.) Both of her flatmates abandoned her in their apartment within the last few weeks. One of them left with a cheery byebye to go back to her parents down south; the other one vanished without a farewell or notice. It's astonishing how fickle people can be. Ruby-Rose had thought that they were her real friends. When calamity explodes, it's easier for many folks to turn selfish and secure their own safety before anything else. She herself can't simply go home to her parents. Because they live in a different country. Overseas. ... But she's doing fine enough. There's enough food in the flat. And she's always been skinny and never much of an eater. And she needn't worry about finance because, to be blunt, her parents are rich and have paid for her tuition fees and have provided a hefty lump of money for her to focus on her studies ... Umm, but yes, it's been mindbending, to isolate in this apartment. ... She remembers those initial days, during the heatwave of late August, when millions got worried about their money and then the worst thing happened. But the temperature dipped mid-September and she thought the Men in Charge would've had a handle of it now. She's still anticipating that the authorities will reign in order. Only she's been thinking that for quite a while and it just keeps going on. ... Every night, before she tries to sleep, she keeps a bag of things ready for her, in case she needs to go, by the front door. Food, water, a sleeping bag, a toiletry bag, etc. Her apartment is high up and has a spanning view of the metropolis from the living room windows. She's seen smoke pluming, miles off. Heard the sirens. As yet it hasn't invaded this part of town. ... She reads books for epic periods and the words take her to different galaxies and they help. (And her flatmates have left their own bookshelves untouched so she helps herself to them too. Ha. And when she reads she likes to make notes and underline/highlight bits amid the text, and doesn't worry whether they'll be angry if they ever come back and find them all annotated and studied.) … Ultimately, Ruby-Rose's plan is to wait it all out. Try and be patient. Not be infected by panic.

MARVIN

It gets to around noon. Marvin has been walking for an age. He's in an intricate claustrophobic area; alleyways, old paths, out-of-date tenements. In the bins below the buildings there are seagulls bickering and scavenging over what foodwaste can still be found. There's an episode where Marvin turns a corner and the gulls must've found something juicy because they all go crazy and yap and squeal and rush over to this single bin looking for what it is. And they outnumber Marvin by thirty and it's actually quite intimidating with them whooshing about and he ducks down and scurries out of there and gets to a new alley with nice cobbles underfoot, where the peasants would've walked two hundred years back. Passes a number of bars which have shuttered their windows up. Finds a lengthy staircase with dark green steps and when he gets to the top he's shorn of breath. He dries his temples and rests for a while. In front of him is a superb church. With that sooty masonry from the industrial age and a witch's-hat spire and these gargantuan oak doors which are bolted in. Everything about the building is impressive. And yet the cross, at the very top of the spire, is so small it's hard to discern from the bottom.

Marvin moves on. He drinks a bit of water and his bottle is kinda running low so he should look into topping it up somewhere … And as he's thinking about that he turns into a new street, which is more like a square, actually, behind the back of the church. And in his reverie he runs right into it.

A police car. It's sitting parked in the square, within calling distance. And it has his back to him. I.e., he's come up on its rear. But he can see two heads through the back window, sitting in the front seats. … And he stops. And turns around, and walks away. *Because if they search me – which they most likely will – they'll find the handgun and then I'm completely doomed.* Marvin tries to seem casual about it and boyishly hopes that they haven't seen him in their mirrors. Then he hears a scratching sound, and turns, and one of the policemen gets out of the car – and he stands up and calls to Marvin:

"Hello, sir."

"Afternoon, sir," Marvin responds, "I'm just on my way this way."

"Where are you off to?"

"Just this way. Minding my own business is all."

"Could you stop for a moment?"

"I'm honestly just on my way home. No problem with me."

"*I'm* telling you to stop, for a second."

Marvin has almost reached the corner. The policemen shouts at him. Marvin bolts. The policeman slaps the door shut. And then shortly after, after he's ran around the corner of the church, he hears the other car door slapping shut. He aims for that staircase again because that's the first opening that's available and he gets to the top and it's rather a steep affair and the steps thin and he hesitates there, fretting that he might fall ... but then the two cops veer round the church corner, and see him and bellow at him to halt and so he hurtles down. ... He's fortunate that his boots have good grip; the stone is worn and marblelike and he wildly aims at jumping down a trio or quartet of the steps at a time as if he's playing some kinda ludicrous game. And throughout this the policemen grunt and gargle and from his peripheral vision they're being cautious in their descent for fear of slipping. ... Marvin reaches the bottom. They trundle down after him. The stairwell has a long wall aside it, so he'll have a useful amount of time to break away from them. He picks an alleyway and dashes down it. Just as he gets to its entrance, the police arrive at the bottom of their bit. They see him. Not over yet. He pelts. And takes the first right he finds and he just uses all the pace he has to get to the climax of this lane and then he turns into another, to a left, and realises that he shouldn't have used up all his horsepower and that he can't keep going without being caught. ... And nearby him is one of those big streetbins from before. And he's already startled the gulls by his panicky appearance and they're hovering above irritably. And an idea shines. He runs over to the bin. Which is jutted just in front of the wall. And he heaves it forward a tad. So he can slip behind it. And then he takes off his backpack and throws it into the gap. And then he crouches down and sits inside there himself. A gamble. Hiding, in an utterly crude way. But it might work. They might not find him. And if they do, then he still has his handgun ... ...

He needn't wait long for the policemen to arrive after him because they're right there, a jumble of metres away, and they jostle and wheeze, *seething* – they're looking to nab him for revenge, having caused all this effort;

"Where is this bastard," one goes.

"He's up there."

"Where!"

"I think I just saw him up that way."

"You sure?"

"Let's get him."

Their boots hammer away in a relieving diminuendo. And Marvin remains under this bin. Shuttered into this position. The sheer *stench* of the bin is overpowering. A whole mix of rancid smells coming from the slat at the top which he can't even place the resource of, wow. He gags. And perhaps he should stay here for a period in case the cops come back, but he keeps gagging and he might retch what little he has in his innards left and so he pushes the bin away from him and gets his bag and then stands up and heads away. His silly espionage gamble was a result and he's not arrested or hurt. The gulls are still above him and know that he's there and resent his presence; they're just as aggressive as the policemen, only smaller. … Marvin chooses a new alley. The other direction of where the cops ran. He jogs into it. Perpetually lost but still surviving.

ELISA

She likes the spot under the bridge and so she stays there for a while. She notices there are pathways either side of the bridge. These tiny trails in the weeds, ever so faint. They haven't been used in some time. But they *used* to be. And it gets her intrigued, and she must be on with her journey. So the river peels away in either direction and the banksides are severed away from the urbanity ahead. She chooses the trail to the north. Not that she has a compass or anything but that's her general direction. And goes along by the riverbank. It's merry. The ferns are browning with the elder autumn. And the thorns are weary too but still way thick and mazy and Elisa wonders what'd be like to be an insect within that heavy mesh. ... And the trail, as she perseveres, grows more prominent and it must lead somewhere. Right enough, she comes across this board. As in, a plaque-like object by the riverside. And views it. It's a map. Elisa's accidentally found a hiking trail or cycling trail. And it leads right up in the northern direction she's after. For quite a decent set of miles. Brilliant. Convenient. From the map it looks like there is woodland following the river, from which she can avoid people in the city.

Elisa ventures.

The sky bruises. Then it begins to rain. Spittery at first. The whisps whisk her face. Then it gets heavier and she puts her hood up. And all the time the valleysides steepen aside her and the river welcomes the rainwater and then the trees sprout up and make the whole scene darker with their trunks and leaves.

Inside the woods the clouds properly break and then suddenly she's in the onslaught of a storm. Must find shelter. She finds this elm tree which still has a good amount of foliage on it and hopes that it might help. It doesn't, at least not for very long. And the pounding on the riversurface makes her nervous and so she heads into the forest. ... Her jeans are already soaked by now. Boots too, she can feel the water in her socks. She edges along the valley and through the thrashing dimness she sees new shapes arching over the river. Crags. Big bunches of rock. She goes down to them and then she descends the bank and indeed this rockface hangs over the water. She treads over the growth and gets under them and the rock texture under her soles are comforting and she just sits down. In this half-cave. The sounds of the rain are alternate here, alien, mystical. Elisa undoes her bag and brings out the one towel she has and she dries her hair. … She shivers. She takes her main coat off and puts it aside and then she takes her boots off and socks off and tries to dry the latter with the towel. She has a spare pair of socks in her bag and she puts those on and then she sees the cans of soup in her bag as well and so she grabs one of them – she needs food to warm her up, and clacks it open and drinks it down. The earthy power of the lentils bulge her tonsils. … Then she remembers her diary. And fears that it might've got soaked by the rain! And checks. But, no. It's fine. She already keeps it in a bandana, and it's unscathed by the dampness. In fact, most of the things in her bag are all right. Elisa can calm down for now. The soup's made her a bit gloopy. And she puts her main coat over her, to act as a cover, and sits against the wall behind her. And it's no situation to rest in at all. But she can wait for the storm to pass, and progress when it's finished.

ANTHONY BURTON

He drives along the motorway. For a solid hour and he's thinking he's making decent ground. Then it starts to rain. And his natural instinct is to turn his windscreen wipers on. And so he does this automatically. Then, of course, the wipers get snagged on the massive indent on his windscreen; they jar there and quiver like dogs and have difficulty moving past it. *Fuck. Those idiot toerags. I bet they would've liked to see the van crash after they hurled that cone. I understand that kids can be cruel, but, crikey, that was madness.* So he quits with the wipers for just now and he focuses extra hard on the road, which is direct and mundane. *Maybe the rain will subside.* It only resurges, just after this sentence has passed in his head, as if the rain had just heard it. And it's getting too dangerous to drive now; the water is worse than the cone-smash damage. *I can't have come all this way just to kill myself in a disaster. Need to find a place to lay off the highway for now.* So he slows his mph and looks out for turn offs from the main route. There's a turquoise sign by the motorway, with white lettering, proclaiming some provincial town, 17 miles down that way. That'll do. He turns off the motorway and heads down it, and very soon he's winding through punky patches of forest and unmanned fields, and it all has a vibe of desolation. Anthony pulls his van off into a mound off the track, under some trees.

Maybe it won't be so bad to get some rest for now. Was feeling sleepy anyway. He stocks up his pipebowl and lights it. And listens to the thundery spitspat of the raindrops on the roof of his van. He doubts that anybody will find him here. Why not just dose in the van for a period? He has a bag of food behind his seat. Takes a can of baked beans from it. (He did make some sandwiches for the voyage but he opts for the sugary savoury protein of some factorycan beans). Eats them with a spoon. He has a blanket in the back too and he puts it over himself. It smells like his apartment, the fabric. He falls asleep.

Anthony Burton dreams.

In the dream he's with his father and they're in a sunny park and both of them are naked at the torso. As in, they're wearing shorts and they're walking down to this amazingly pristine lake, with ducks and those rubbery strands of grass at the base. Dad puts a bunch of towels down before them on the bankside and then he steps confidently into the water and he tells Anthony to do the same. Anthony does so and tries not to show that the cold smarts him. Dad then takes it further by delving into the water, full-body: he plunges his head under the surface and then lifts it up and his locks are all wild and big face blinking by emergence. Anthony watches him, still only at his ankles. "Be brave, Tony," his father says, and then turns around and launches into the water and begins swimming. Away from him. Broadstroke. ... Anthony takes this as the message to follow. So he proceeds and the pebbles and grit are rough and he gets to his shins and then the water's deep enough to jump into and yet he's too scared and so he gets to his thighs and then the liquid reaches his scrotum and penis and it's as if the both of them shrivel up instantaneously and that's the worst bit and so he just rushes in and his lungs blaze from the cool as well and momentum tells him to start swimming. An art he was never skilful at. He prefers a frontcrawl himself, and makes to catch up with his father, who's already way far into the lake. ... At first the episode is all exhilarating. Until his father is going too fast and only focusing on his own swimming. "Dad," Anthony calls out to him, "Dad, can you slow down please?" Father either doesn't hear him or just ignores him. And then Anthony knows that he's gone way far into the lake and he's scared to go any further. So he turns back. But then, *what if Dad thinks less of me for not being able to match him?* So he tries again, to swim and swim. And very quickly he starts failing. His muscles sag and he panics, and with the panic his chest moves irrationally and he loses oxygen and then his face starts dipping under the water and it fills his mouth. He swallows. Coughs. He vomits it out. "Father. Dad! I'm in trouble! Help me!"

Anthony wakes up.

There is a pinkness in the sky. And it's stopped raining.

He can't think how to analyse that dream. He barely ever dreams about his Dad, who passed away when Anthony was much younger.

It's around six thirty in the morning. He should look to be getting back on the motorway. Anthony smokes some of his pipe, but only gets half-way through it – it doesn't work for him this morning. Then he drives on back up this sideroad and finds the motorway in swift timing and then he flumes down that. ...

The light of the morning ascends as he goes. It's like diving into a painting whilst it's being painted. With these streaks changing in the sky, all brightening in a mass canvass. He imagines he's on a fair romp. Refreshed. The road is still wet but it has a nice glimmer to it as if it were waving heat. … Anthony turns a corner and then spots something in the distance. Something blocking the road, and he cools the velocity.

Takes him a while to interpret the scene.

Police vans. They've blocked off both this lane of the motorway and the adjacent one also. With their vans, which there are about ten of. And it looks as if they're setting up some type of barricade across the motorway. Anthony has approached them and the policemen, scores of them, are looking at him. And he's paused there in the road not knowing what to do or what this all means. He certainly won't be able to go on physically because they've already erected much of the barricade. But why are they building it anyway? What's the point of this? … And as Anthony's stationed there, this one policeman walks towards his van. With a wild fluorescence brimming even in the emerging daylight. Anthony needs to stop being gullible, pay attention. So he waves to the policeman nearing him. Which is lame. The policeman doesn't wave back. He's young, with a clean jaw – the cop – and Anthony opens his door and gets out into the air. He shuts his door and the policeman calls Hi.

"Good morning, sir," Anthony says.

"Hello there. What are you doing out here?" the cop arriving close by him. Alert eyes. Prickly posture.

"I was just trying to head north."

"You can't go this way I'm afraid. Motorway is closed off at this point."

"Why?"

"We can't let any vehicle through, I'm sorry."

"But why are you barricading it? I don't understand."

"We can't give out information."

"Ehh, well. Do you know if there's another route I can take nearby?"

"No, I'm not familiar. You can find out elsewhere though."

The policeman looks up at Anthony's windscreen.

"What happened there?"

"Oh … It was some kids. They threw something from an overpass. Whilst I was on my way here actually. A traffic cone … Chucked it from the top of the pass."

"Why didn't you report this?"

"I don't know … I, uh. I'm in a hurry. I can still drive."

"You can?"

"Yes."

"But you know it's illegal to be driving with a smashed windscreen …"

Anthony nods.

"I haven't had time to get it fixed yet, sir."

"Well, what I'm saying to you this morning, is, that you should head back the way you came. Because you can't pass through this way. And try get your window fixed. Right?"

"Okay."

"I could just as easily take you in right now and write you up for illegal driving. Do you want that?"

"No, right, okay, thank you, I get you."

"Good. So you'll be on your way as of now, uh hu?"

"Yes sir, I will. Thanks."

Anthony gets back in his van. The cop walks back to his colleagues triumphantly. Not even smug, just victorious. Anthony makes a U-turn with his van, and drives onwards, watching the police barricade in his mirrors with an elastic civilian rage. Which he can do nothing about. He must obey.

RUBY-ROSE

The crisis has affected her sleep a lot. She used to be a fairly normal sleeper, as in, before midnight and a clean break until the late a.m. hours – one of those lucky people. But with nothing to do and being unable to go outside her sleeping has changed and she doesn't notice how it's altering her mentality. Ruby-Rose is not depressed or anxious by sleeping less. She tends to nap in the late afternoons and then stay up until the dark mornings wherein there's a loud hush and she pulls her curtains shut and reads and it's like being somewhere else entirely. So she's sleeping about a third less than what she used to. Hypnotic, would be a possible word. Her experience of sentience is changing; light and shade are sharper, the letters on the pages of her books are vivid symbols. Noises are profound.

For instance, there was a moment on one of these surreal late nights when she was reading. And this intense buzzing came above her on the ceiling and she got this incredible fright. A wasp. It was just a wasp. And she had a mild fear of those insects just like anybody does but not a phobia. The *sound* was mammoth and she just sat there blinking at it – could hear its wings and its confused plops and bumps as it hit the walls looking for a way out. (It was one of those morbid Autumnal wasps which seek heat indoors because winter is looming outside, and it's naively believing in immortality.) So Ruby-Rose left the room and read in the kitchen instead and then fell asleep on the living room couch, because she could not handle the audio of that flying thing. And when she returned to her bedroom next day the wasp had shrivelled and died on her desk and she felt sorry for it and she scooped it up on a post-it note and opened the window and tossed it out and the wind took its body and hurled it away unto the metropolis.

It's October now. The month has just turned and her situation remains the same. Waiting. Without any signs of the State intervening in this grand mess.

Within these late hours, before she finally goes to sleep she usually makes a tomato sauce and pasta. Likes the way the steam plays on the windows: and she draws little pics on the glass with her fingers. Likes the food too, reminds her of home. Albeit her mother's tom sauce was hands down worldclass and way better than hers. ... So she's tired of reading tonight and she puts her dressing gown on and goes into the kitchen to make some food and she boils the kettle. Then starts slicing the onions. Rash luscious smell. … Before the windows steam up they show her reflection. She's quite tall for a young woman; has these stout legs and these light shoulderblades and her nose is rather angelic. The kettle finishes and she pours it in the pot and turns the gas on. And even that small hissing is way too loud so she turns it on lowest mark. … Then there is this other noise which comes from elsewhere in the small world of her flat.

From out in the street. Her knife stops cutting. And she listens and watches the window, whereupon her face is frozen in the reflection. Yes, there's definitely something happening outside. She turns the gas off. Then the lights off in the kitchen: because she knows her light can be seen from the streetview. Puts the knife down and goes through to the living room and there she peers out of the windows there.

She can see down onto the final part of the road. There are a group of people there. A lot of them. Maybe eight, nine of them – their bodies are fluttering shapes and they walk without coordination and she can hear them calling. Not shouting but not speaking casually either. They're next to the group of shops. … There's the hardware store, the sports shop and the café by that, from what she can make out at this distance. (She used to go to the café a lot before the Crash. Doesn't know the sports one or hardware.) Ruby-Rose watches the group, pack, gang, in total dark, awkwardly perched on her knees by the window. The group just hang there as if it's daylight and they're socialising or waiting for something. Expecting. … And it turns out that they are. Because ten minutes later a new group arrive. Doubling the gang population. And what's more: they're pushing trolleys in front of them. Standard supermarket trolleys.

Ruby-Rose is transfixed.

The figures with the trolleys greet them all. Inside the trolley-baskets are items which she can't see from this range – she cannot really see them so clearly and it's like watching animate toy soldiers. Action commences. They pick up these items from the trolleys. And attack the hardware store. Bricks? They lob them at the windows of the hardware shop and the smash sounds are muffled through Ruby's own window. They throw and throw at the windows until the sheets buckle apart and collapse in a mass sheet of glass. And then the mob storm the store. They hob gleefully over the glass and in through the new gap … and disappear inside, and then re-emerge in groups, carrying bundles of goods in their arms. Which they place into the trolleys.

There are many stark, factual commands, as if they were a workforce in a factory. They're efficient and fast in the same way, loading up the trolleys with the hardware equipment. All they can fit in to the cages. … But not all of them – the trolleys – they're saving a few aside and not filling those ones up and Ruby-Rose wonders why. Until the gang start picking up the bricks again: and begin chucking them at the sports shop. They chuck and chuck and chuck and the front window of this place seems tougher because they can't break through it, and by their frenzied body movements it's obvious they're getting annoyed about it. … So they give up. On it. And out of petulance then they turn their attention to the café, whose window bursts easily. They ransack this sad coffeeshop … and Ruby-Rose thinks *why would they want to loot a café? It's just a tiny coffeeshop with nothing valuable in it?* And yet the mob lug out a handful of bulky material, which isn't enough to fill the remaining trolleys. And so the pack make do with what they have and they escape, rolling their cages along, with screeches and hoots … and they leave a bundle of the trolleys behind, who sit there amid the debris as if abandoned and upset.

Throughout the whole incident not one light has sparked on throughout the entire flat block in front of her, or any down the street. If anybody is still here, they're like her: they are too afraid to do anything.

Ruby-Rose's kneecaps have gone all icy.

She stands up and sits on her couch and she has never seen such violence before. Real violence that is. It's far different from films, she now knows. She's still in blackness and now her flat has entered a new chapter. One of which she must end soon. She's the protagonist of this chapter and she dislikes the role.

I must leave this apartment. Can't stay here. The rioting and looting, anarchy, whatever you want to call it, has finally come to my district and I'm too scared of it. Why procrastinate? In the morning I should take my bag and my bike and leave. I don't have a plan but I have money and I can take food with me. I'm a strong cyclist and can go fast. Wait until daylight. Leave then. If I can just get to a safer part of the city. Or find a motel on the outskirts or something like that or even just camp out for a while … I can't go mad in this place. They'll come back tomorrow. They'll invade the other shops down the street and then they'll come in here and rampage me. A rich girl like me – they won't take any pity on me and they'll rob me and even worse.

She re-catches a whiff of onions from the kitchen. Panic's overriding her consciousness and she must concentrate on something else. So gets up and gets back in the kitchen.

There's no point in making the pasta sauce anymore. But she can make some rolls. Ruby-Rose is neat with a humous and salad roll. (At least she likes them.) And so she goes into the bottom-fridge cabinet and plucks tomatoes and cucumber and she already has a bit of the lettuce and she does the rolls up and slurps humous on them and wraps them in cellophane and sticks them all, save one, in a bag, and puts this into her main rucksack which is at the main door. Then she eats the roll she saved.

Then brings her bike out from the end of the corridor. She's missed cycling for the past five weeks, and inspects the bicycle to make sure that it's all okay and ready for travelling. Looks good. And as ludicrous as the situation is, she's actually looking forward to some kind of adventure tomorrow.

But she should try and get some rest, if she can. And she heads into her bedroom and the air is warmer at least and the lamplight a soft vermillion. She's still wearing her main clothes. Jeans and a jumper. And she should probably shower in order to get ready. But she's just way too fatigued. So she strips off down to complete nakedness (which is usually how she sleeps) and gets into bed. And yet, when she turns her lamp off and relaxes on the pillow, her mind is too jarred to ease down. Her imagination can't stop. She lies there for far too long, not being able to shut down. So she gets up again. *Maybe sleep isn't that important.* She heads through to the bathroom and switches the light on and she's ready for its blare and she whacks the shower on and the flat's lucky enough to have a powerful shower and she hops up onto the tub and into the hot wild liquid.

MARVIN

Marvin comes upon a promenade and he takes a breather and he sits on the curb by the pavement. He's high up in the city. It's mature afternoon and white skied and quite warm. And from here he can see the skyscrapers. Far far away to the south, in the city centre by the river. The famous outlines of them, that is. Despite having lived here all his life Marvin's never been close to them physically. He knows them as a native, a vision. But they've never seemed lofty or beautiful to him before and they don't now – they only seem banished and ironic. Ironic icons. And of course a lot of those buildings are corporate offices, banking/financial hubs, FatCat structures. Directly involved in the Crash. ... Marvin imagines that he has a rocket launcher and that he stands up and aims at the scrapers and fires and watches the rockets sail across the sky and hit the buildings with fiery brilliance. Just a boyish sliver of fantasy. He alights from the curb and goes on.

He finds himself in a neighbourhood of terrace housing which he's utterly unfamiliar with. The walls of the houses are brown and zigzag skilfully up the mounds and slopes of the roads, which as he walks up and down become quickly tight and he can't suss whether any people are here and whether anybody such as himself would be welcome if indeed he gets caught out as a stranger. Chimneys and satellite dishes keep churning on and on, Marvin walking in a video replay. And he worries that he might get lost or that he's already lost.

Inky crows perch on the rooftops too and pretend that they're not looking at him.

All this labyrinthian time he's seen nothing moving on the roads before him and then there is this one jittery sight on this new street and it makes him jump and he crouches down. It's a cat. Twenty times smaller than him and nowhere near him and yet it made him wince. ... He pauses and watches it. It has grey fur and it jumps up onto one of the walls before a house and sits there, still not knowing that Marvin is there: he or she hasn't seen him yet.

He approaches coyly. Marvin didn't have a pet animal when he was a kid, or ever, and he never thought about them much, the same way as he doesn't find babies or children cute. Suddenly, though, this animal intrigues him. ... It sees him. And its reaction is to bolt down the wall and down the pavement and rip up onto the wall, again, farther down the way. Then it stops and peers at Marvin. It wears a collar and so it's obviously a housecat. *So did somebody abandon it? I haven't seen any trace of life here and have passed a hundred houses. Did one of the families leave their cat behind! That's not fine.* He walks closer and the cat just stays there on the wall, watching but curious also. Then its tail fattens and it tautens and looks like it might run away. Marvin notices that it's very thin. Pities it. He thinks it's going to flee him and he walks on and on and it still doesn't move and then its tail softens and it sits … and Marvin says, speaks out to this creature:

"I'm not going to hurt you, cat," and it's strange and almost embarrassing to hear his voice in this environment.

The cat stays mute. He thinks maybe it could do with some food. Marvin is not going to take this cat with him out of the city but perhaps he could help it out one last time before it starves to death. … So he reaches into his bag and finds one of the tins of mackerel. That he has. Oily fish. Surely a cat would like that if it is ravenous and starving. … Marvin opens the tin and that gaudy scent pips up in the air and he holds it out to the cat. Who doesn't budge. So he walks towards the cat and then the cat leaps off and up to the door of the house. "I just wanted to give you some food, if you want it," Marvin says, and he leaves the tin on the wall where the cat just was. … The feline is still resilient and won't come close. "Well," Marvin says, "It's there if you want it." And he walks on. And completes the street and he looks back at that spot on the wall. Hovers there. … And eventually the cat jumps back up, thinking Marvin's gone. And it tucks in to the can of fish. Jaws chomping.

It's crucial to be kind. Small pots of kindness can enrich a being. Even if they aren't heavy pots, or if they don't look ornamental, if they aren't long-term.

Marvin gave the can of mackerel to the cat as a short term gift. It's probable that the cat won't find anything else as lucky anytime soon and it'll have to hunt for mice from now on. But that was a trade of rare grace. To have one's power to do something beneficial for another, even if it's a doomed housecat. To be decent, show goodwill. Why *not* show grace, or deal it, fashion it? Marvin is glad that with all he's witnessed recently that he can chose to have heart. Hold hope … He salutes the cat and switches back onto the trail with vigour. He comes out at the top of a final mound, where the neighbourhood ends and the tarmac tone in the roads change and there's a bus shelter nearby and he goes in there and checks the map. As in, the details for the bus times (which obviously are now useless) and the map next to it, and he's surprised by the sight of the location, that he's come this far. He has no clue where he'll sleep tonight or if that will happen at all. He's not that fretful though. For a while he sits on the bus shelter bench. The afternoon tinge in the sky slowly darkens.

ELISA

There's a long time before it stops raining and when it finally does it is night time. Elisa has managed to dose a little, in dreary baffled bouts. Her body is astonishingly frail, she feels, as she stands up and puts her coat around her and zips it up … as if, were she to fall on the crags she might smash like a lightbulb and never be able to piece herself up again. She's careful therefore to pick her way down the rocks and back into the weeds.

The forest is decimated by the rain. It's ripped much foliage from the trees, flattened the brush, blackened the bark. Elisa can see almost nothing. She holds her arms out in front of her as she walks to avoid hitting anything. She must find that hiking/cycle trail again so she can reconvene with her own trek … and there is a period where she frets she won't get back to it again, such is the bewilderment of her surroundings … but she discovers it far quicker than expected: she thought she'd derailed from the path a great distance. Perhaps it was the mania of the rain that made her think so. Anyway, she's back. She makes strong progress. The night clouds somehow have the smallest amount of light for her to see the trail, who knows from what source, perhaps the universe beyond them. …

Elisa notices that the trees disperse and the river turns a different direction from the trail and doesn't come back again and then there is an urban light on the horizon. What is it? Another bridge? A green-yellow haze which destroys all the mysticism of the woodland. She must confront it. It's not a bridge but a new gabble of houses. Rather nice ones. Quite like cottages, or wealthy abodes and their windows are black but the lanterns on the pathway give off a classical vibe, and the trail then leads up and up and comes out onto a road and it's surreal to feel concrete under her soles again, as if she's never experienced it before. It's actually comforting and then the road dips down again and there is further municipal gleaming at the bottom of the hill.

Three tenement flats; council buildings, an estate. The gleam not from the buildings but the streetlamps – which are archaic, a kind she hasn't met before – and she keeps to the main road because she doesn't want to go into this block, wherever it is: she has no clue where she is in the city, not exactly.

But then as she pursues she comes upon something unusual.

A car. Up ahead on the road. Parked there. Normally, just the single car. And Elisa thinks *maybe somebody's alive out here? Nearby – still around? Or are they maybe in the car?* She pauses and analyses it for a while. What makes this vehicle different is that it's the first one she's seen intact within weeks; all the others burnt out or bashed beyond oblivion. *If there are people in there – can they help me? I still only have the one can of soup left. I don't know what else I can do for food.* She walks forward. And gets to the vehicle and there is nobody in it. It's red. Cheap un-flashy car, simple. And this great yearning rushes in her breast, that she wishes she were an adult and that she could drive, knew how to drive, and that she could escape fast and never return. Elisa wonders what she'll look like as an adult … The way it's looking with her situation, she probably won't get to such an age. She hasn't even hit puberty yet.

The vehicle can't help her and even if it is useable, the owner might not want her snooping around it, and could appear any moment – who knows where he or she could be – and so she leaves it.

A small breeze, temperature in low Celsius, below five at least … She keeps her nose down as she walks.

Roundabout. A roundabout appears, vast, with three separate main roads to choose from.

Which way do I go now? The roundabout is stark and the trio of routes brazen … She decides to go straight on, pick the same direction she's been going all the time, despite the distortion of the passes.

Roundabouts used to scare her because they were always super fast and whirly and she used to pass one every day on the bus to school and she'd turn her eyes away from the windows as the bus reeled round it – dangerous with the convoluted traffic, and she feared that a cyclist would get mashed or that vehicles would bash into each other. … And it's phobic to walk across this roundabout in the chilly gloom without any sound or movement and she passes to the island-bit in the middle of it where the grass is silky and she gets beyond that and then sees a shape lying on the floor of the road she's just arrived at.

Person. A body. It's definitely a body. Elisa can't tell whether it's male or female but it's wearing a cyan raincoat and winterboots and it's on its front and one of the arms is sprawled out at an awry angle. Did they get run over? And were left here, classic hit and run? … Elisa ponders whether she should say something or make a prayer, an ode to that affect. She hasn't the wisdom for it, aside from, in her head, *I hope it wasn't sore*, and she has to get closer to the body because that's where she's headed and has to pass this shape and she can't look at it either and Elisa is able to turn her eyes but she can't evade the smell of it and the instant she gets a whiff it makes her gag and she gets a second powerful guff in her mouth and she dry wretches and then begins jogging to bail from that rampant stench.

Elisa coughs and her eyes are wincing for an age after she's passed on from the body. Lingering. The night shows no care for anything. She's under a curtain, the fabric of it dense. Will it ever be lifted? Or will she lie here, be stuck here, forever?

ANTHONY BURTON

That dream he had about his father has got him thinking. A whole fleet of memories wave and wander as he's driving his van along this new motorway.

Anthony's father, Cecil, was a peculiar man. He was often silent, fixated on his own planet. Not a bad father by any means – he was just hard to communicate with, didn't have friends, go to parties. Which was odd because his wife, Mandy, Anthony's mother, was quite the extrovert and did do all of those things every weekend. Cecil was well-paid, a scientific chap who worked for a corporation, long hours a week right up until he died; left early in the morning and came home at seven p.m., that archetypal kinda nuclear family deal. Except Anthony was their only child, and, expect they were not a normal family. Mandy would often shout at Cecil. These furious hectic garrulous tantrums; would explode at him and Cecil would rarely ever respond to her, only sit there and take it as if he was her child. … And often it was in front of Anthony. Who was blistered by these onslaughts and did not understand the situations in any way, often didn't know what she was on about, or get the jargon that she used. … From what Anthony recalls as an adult, Mandy often complained/shouted/raged about Cecil's profession. On a standard basis that he was more interested in his work than his family. But there was something else. And extra ingredient which made her so angry. Because she would say things like; "You're employed by *them*! Those greedy fiends!", "You sell your soul to people like that and lap up their money!" … Such sentences. Anthony still doesn't know what his father's role was; although he does know the corporation and it's a famous one, internationally huge. A disliked one. Responsible for much global atrocity. So was that what Mandy was wrathful about? Maybe. Either way, Anthony's childhood wasn't so irate compared to some examples. Upper Middle Class (whatever strata you want to put him in, if you take 'class' terms seriously) and lived in a suburb in a full house with superfluous rooms. Anthony had lots of toys. His parents were close most of the time and they seemed to make up quickly after a scorching Mandy episode. They'd go out on weekend nights and hire this babysitter. (Who was this late-teen from down the road called Sarah, whom Anthony quickly developed a crush for. She had stunning hair. She made him food and let him watch movies, even the adult-certificate ones his parents wouldn't allow him to watch, and he enjoyed her and missed her when she went off to university and didn't come back to the suburb again.)

Yes, Cecil didn't speak much to Anthony. He liked to *teach* rather than talk. On weekend afternoons Cecil would often be in the garden shed, making stuff with tools. Inventing. Carpentry especially. And he'd show Anthony how to hammer, saw, burn, file and so on. Anthony couldn't keep at his same speed but he loved the tutorials and was keen to impress his father. ... And to this day there's a small shame within him that he was never able to match his father's genius – even if that sounds lame. Because Anthony looks over his own life and he's been moderately successful. But not like his Dad. Even though he still doesn't know Cecil's full story. ... When Anthony was a kid, the economy was totally different and Cecil would be considered rich in today's equivalence, if compared. ... Cecil died of a stroke at the age of 45. Even that was mysterious. Because he was a man who didn't drink or smoke or eat badly. This happened when Anthony was a student and he got the news when he was studying for his exams. ... And came back to the suburb – the hospital nearest that – and took the train and it was December and nearing Christmas and the fields were all full of moonlit snow and he got to the hospital without having heard any news for hours and Mandy met him in the reception area and she said, "Your Pop hasn't made it." ... ... Anthony could not believe it. Where on earth he developed a lethal stroke from bemused everybody. But it happened. ... As Anthony thinks about him now there is this one prominent theme of memory. A gabble of scenes which were very similar. They also occurred in boyhood. It was when Anthony was getting ready to go to school in the mornings. (A place which he hated.) When he went down to the kitchen for breakfast, Cecil would be reading the newspaper, without fail. Studiously fascinated by the small text of the broadsheet. Cecil wouldn't say Hi or even acknowledge his son and Anthony would put a pair of bread slices in the toaster, butter and jam, nervous about getting bullied at school and sit there on the table, watching his father. ... Then Cecil would place his paper down. And drink some of his coffee. And say, "This world is going to self-destruct one day, son. You're going to have to do something about it when you're older." And Anthony wouldn't know what he meant. Cecil honestly said that pair of lines so many times, unaware that he was repeating himself. And there was a single occasion where Anthony spoke back to him, where he said,

"What do you mean Dad? What can I do about the world?"

"You'll be involved in it, son."

"But what will happen?"

"I don't know. But it'll be bad. You need to be prepared."

"How do I do that? Please tell me what you mean."

"You've got talent, son. That'll be the way you find your way out of it. It's not you personally that will cause it all. But I'm predicting self-destruction. For this society. I'm warning you that you'll have to brace yourself for it."

And Anthony was seven years old when Cecil said all that him, and the dialogue terrorized him so much that he chose not to respond when Cecil delivered those words again, countless times afterwards:

This world is going to self-destruct one day, son. You're going to have to do something about it when you're older.

Anthony finally understands that his father was right.

He's been angry with his Dad all his life for saying that to him as a kid. For using that type of language with a child's mind, which cannot comprehend. And he's still angry with him, because his predictions were correct: Anthony simply didn't want to believe in his madness for all this time. And nor did Cecil ever give him any solid advice. Just those witchy wizardly comments instead. How were they supposed to 'prepare' Anthony?

Perhaps they have,

It's early afternoon and Anthony has sussed out another direction up north. An alternate motorway. … His van's still operable and he has hope. His parents are gone (Mandy dead as well). Why still think about them? Even though they bore him. He'll have to deal with this alone.

RUBY-ROSE

Ruby-Rose checks her things. She puts her dear belongings in the upper/inner pocket of her bag. There's a gem stone which her best friend (who was called Emma) from back home (home country) gave her when they were girls and she would never leave it here. She puts it in the pouch along with this necklace which she adores and this mini-deck of cards she's had, which she also played with Emma whence wee.

There's this one problem she's had all morning which is driving her nuts. She can't find her bike helmet. Which is odd because everything else about her bicycle is all perfect and geared up to voyage. *Where the fuck is my helmet?* She searches all over the flat and it makes no cameo. Despite everything universal going on and the danger outside and uncertainty of the future, this helmet thing annoys her … until she remembers. She recollects the last time she must've had it. Which was right before the Crash. Right before the economy was decapitated, she cycled around to her friend's house, one of her university chums, a few clicks away in the city. Just to hang out. (They watched a movie and Ruby-Rose's friend talked about this boy on campus that she couldn't stop looking at.) … Friendly normal stuff like that. And then two days later history occurred. Umm, and Ruby-Rose hasn't used her bike since that time. So she must have left it at her friend's house. Oh well. Zilch she can do about it. She'll have to embark onwards without a helmet.

It's a shiny morning. Not clear-skied exactly but there is a wide shine from her windows. She locks all the windows. Turns off the electrical appliances in the kitchen, switches off all the plugs. … There's a painting which she's fond of on the kitchen wall above the sink and she can't take it with her because it's too big and the artist is an unjustly underrated one that few people know about and she often points him out to people to turn them on to his stuff; despite him dying prematurely 150 years ago she believes he deserves much more acclaim.

And her flatmate's items are still all there in their rooms, pretty much all their stuff, and Ruby-Rose feels deviant in not protecting it.

She has a wiry body and there's a limit to how much she can carry.

But anyway, she opens her front door and lifts her bike out first and then locks her door and then wheels her bike to the staircase at the end of the corridor and picks it up and takes it down. For some reason she doesn't trust the elevator. Ruby-Rose relishes the initiation of journey, lifting this bicycle down the steps and it's as if being re-charged, from the five week dormant dream she's undergone upstairs.

She gets to the front doors and opens them and this amazing pressure of air bathes her face and she heads into it acceptingly.

It's also startling. The daylight. Berserk as birdsong and yet there are no birds around. Only the crippled street.

She sits on her saddle and sets off. And her way bypasses the wreckage of what she saw last night, with the looting. She has to past by the carnage. *Which looks a lot smaller in the daylight*, she thinks, *the shops, as bust as they are; they're mere boxes, a trifle, a sideshow … Their windows can be restored in the future.* And of course it's all tragic. It's a tiny headline. 50 words in a newspaper article which nobody will ever write. Won't cause any constitutional change.

Ruby-Rose cycles and in order to avoid the glass she cycles on the far pavement and it's surprising how many shards have gotten this distance across the area. And the trolleys – those empty numbers that the gang abandoned in the night – are still there and they watch her pass, still bitter and dejected. She rounds the corner and then she's on the main street. Which is a clean run up for block on block and she pedals and pedals and it's beautiful.

The flags are outside the embassy which stands at the summit of this bit, flowing there modestly. And there's a statue of a famous man, all in chocolaty bronze, a few minutes later. (He's even older than that artist mentioned hitherto. He snuffed it 300 years back.) And she gets into the main district and she passes the subway station, from where a blast of pigeons suddenly bomb. And she isn't expecting them and they make her stop. She laughs, though, over their clumsy ballet. Pigeons have a likeable clumsiness to them and she hasn't experienced that in so long and here she is in the inner city and she's the only person witnessing them. She grins. And as her lips widen her mood lifts higher and she thinks perhaps this mission will end well. And onwards she pedals, and she passes the cinema with its lofty staircase and beyond that the museum with its pillars and down into the plaza of plush restaurants – all of which are ripped up by the riots, and she already knows all of this because she saw it all in the news and so she just chooses not to observe the damage and goes on and on.

Ruby-Rose has a good sense of direction and thus she has her route in her feet, knows which streets to take.

She cuts through many miles in a short time.

And she decides to stop at a point on the street because her legs are tiring. She sets her bicycle by the curb and she un-cellophanes one of her humous rolls and starts eating it. Tomato acid. Shiva cucumber, the handsomeness of bread, earthy peal of chick peas.

A man walks down toward her from the top of the street.

Ruby-Rose has no idea that he's there.

Nor him her. Until he comes past a black bin and sees her and he yells:

"HEY THERE DOLL!"

And it startles her so that she swallows awkwardly and jolts forward at the same time and the food gets stuck in her throat. She gurgles and coughs and her face reddens. And amidst this calamity she looks up and there is this strange man coming nearer with a leering gait. He's drunk. She knows it from the way he moves. Suddenly she's endangered.

She tosses her roll away into the gutter and gets up and zips her bag back up and puts it on and then lifts her bike up and sits on it – her intention being to drive away from this man, whoever he is. … But he's already a few metres from her by the time she's done this and so she stays on the saddle. He's grinning. She can smell him. He wears this winter jacket, green, with the fake furry hood. He must be in his forties; his cheeks are all cratered by historical acne. …

"Hey there doll," he says, "Sorry, I didn't mean to frighten you."

"That's okay."

"I just wanted to say hello to you."

"Hello there, sir."

"You're the only person I've seen in days."

"Yeah me too … I must be on my way now," and she makes to move on with her bike. Her eyelids twitch. He twitches as well, stepping sideways a bit. She hesitates.

"What's your name?"

"Ruby-Rose."

"Hahaha. Is that a real name? Your actual name I mean."

"It is, yes."

"Wow … well, sure is a lovely name. My name's Oli."

"Nice to meet you Oli."

"Your name's almost as beautiful as you are. My o my! Look at that face. You look like an actress: you belong in the movies, honey, I swear."

Ruby-Rose smiles a very grim tight forced smile. He steps towards her a foot and she flinches.

"Why are you scared?" Oli says.

"I'm not. It's just I've got to get on now. Be well now."

"You don't want to stay and talk for a bit?"

"I'm in a rush is all. Nothing personal."

"You're not from around here are you? You're accent's different."

"I'm not from here, no. Ho ho."

Everything is telling her to get on the pedals and zip past and away from him. *So why am I not doing it?*

Oli guesses which country she's from and asks if he is right and Ruby-Rose says yes, you got it.

Then Oli looks down at the roll – the half-eaten one that's now lying in the gutter. And his expression morphs, expands with a swap of interest.

"Have you got any food, honey?" Oli says. "Ruby-Rose? Do you have some food for me? Please I haven't eaten in so long, I'm dying, literally dying. Please!"

And at this point he's come right next to her on the bicycle and her heart yammers. She's thinking – *I can give him one of my other rolls and be charitable and then he will leave me be. Just give him something to eat. Then calmly cycle away and all will be cool.* She takes her bag off and he stares monstrously at it as she does so, mouth drooling, literally, and he breathes on her and his breath is a mix of vomit and something savoury that's gone off. Ruby-Rose does one of her difficult smiles again and she hands a roll out to him. He grabs it.

"Here you go sir, Oli … I hope you like it."

"Oh, honeypie, you are just the best, a total princess!" and he leans forward and kisses her on the cheekbone and the touch is guttural, his lips acidic, and she grimaces. (She wishes she could wipe his saliva off her skin but this would seem provocative and so she doesn't do so.) "Thank you so much."

"No problem. Be well. I wish you all the best, man."

She finally pushes down on the pedals and then thinks that she's free.

Then there's this rough clamp on her forearm and she loses

balance on her bike and has to stop and turns and Oli has a grip of her. He stares right into her, eyeballs pink with booze. His temples sweat. *How did he get any alcohol if he couldn't get any food?*

"You not want to stay and eat with me, Ruby-Rose?"

"I'd like to but, as I say, I'm on a journey here."

"Why you not want to eat with me? I seen you had some more rolls in that bag. Have one with me?"

"Please let go of my arm. It's sore."

Her voice switches up an octave. Oli does not let go. Instead, his jaws clench.

"Just spend some time with me," he seethes, "that's all I'm asking."

And then he clutches her face with his other hand. She panics. And yells:

"I gave you some food! What more do you fucking want!"

Oliver punches her.

Ruby-Rose has never experienced a punch before and it's quite perplexing and then she's on the floor, clumsily entwined with the bicycle and she hits her head when she lands in the concrete, at the corner of the skull, which puts this drowsy douse on everything else which is about to happen. ... Oli rips her body up from the bike and he is enlivened and frenzied and strong and he smacks her down on the pavement again. As yet, she's too dazed to scream. Then he takes a knife out of his pocket. And she squeals. He presses the tip of the blade by her throat, and he whispers, "Don't you *move*, you small whore." ... The knife looks like a common kitchen one you would use to cut ingredients for your evening meal and yet it's right by her eyes and so it looks massive. And this man is about double the weight of her. He's pressing her down easily and she can't get up and she's shouting and shouting please get off don't hurt me please get off and don't do this, don't do it. And she feels this small dribble of urine come out of her vagina. Out of fear. Which hasn't happened since she played Hide-and-Seek when she was like six with her friends, when she was hiding somewhere in a garden at a birthday party and was afraid of being found. ... And then this man, creature, undoes his belt and wrenches his trousers and boxers down and she can see his erect thing. (She's not that familiar with penises but this one looks like an alien deformity rather than an organ.) Then Oliver undoes the upper buttons of her jeans and pulls her panties down afterwards and her thighs are lush and white and ripe. They're like glowing oil paintings, her legs, and yet lively and right at the base of his masculinity. ... All this is happening in direct daylight on the cement of a deserted street. ... Oliver leans back, to prepare himself for the penetration. And as he does so, he leans off her body just a bit, just a tad. And his pathetic genitals are right there in the open. Ruby-Rose sees the chance. And takes it: she kneecaps him in the nuts = as profane as that sounds, that's what she does ... and it works. Because he drops the knife, with the impact. It trundles out of his hand and lies by her left side. And her left arm is suddenly free because he's lost grip of that as well, crumpled by that manhood-blow, and he's clutching his balls. ... And she picks up the knife. She's got it. She's half naked and lying under him and he's now incensed and his erection has dimmed a bit but he's still above her. And he grumbles, "Urgh, you sick bitch: I'll get you now." And he lunges down to her, not noticing that she has the knife. And she switches it, slices it, across his face. ... The impact (what she feels in the texture of her hand) is not much different to slashing vegetables. Only that there is this warm splash which goes across her face and some of it goes in her eye, and then this lumpy mass falls onto her and winds her, takes the oxygen out of her torso.

He's still on top of her and he's bellowing now and mad and hellish and she catches this one sight above him, of his face all besmeared with blood and it's falling on her. And then his hands find her throat and then he presses down with them and he's choking her and she can't intake any air.

And she's still holding the knife and she plucks it up and rams it into his side. Anywhere. Aims for anywhere.

Oliver falls to the side. Not on her. He emits this worn, drawn out groan.

Ruby-Rose stands up and away from him, with her drawers and jeans still down, raw down to the shins. And she pulls her pants up and does her jean buttons up.

The knife is stuck inside Oli's right kidney and he's squatting on the floor, moaning, his face all gory. He's swearing quietly as if he were in slumber and cursing his past demons. She's disarmed him. She feels guilty and wicked.

She gets back to her bike and gets on top of it. Somewhere throughout the fight her bag was knocked off and she doesn't remember when that bit happened and it's lying a few yards away from Oli and so she has to go back and get it and go closer to him again and she can't help but look at that kitchen blade planted in his side and by this point he's flattened on the ground and he's still breathing but unlikely to do much moving from now on. … She gets the bag. Puts it on and saddles her bike and cycles onward and onward.

And the daylight is just as silent and nutritious as ever.

PART TWO

MARVIN

Marvin sleeps in somebody's garden shed after walking for hours in the night. After he's sure nobody's in the house. He sees a shed's roof over a garden fence, no illumination from the house itself and so he climbs up and over and breaks into the shed, which is pretty easily done. And he shuts the door behind him and it's not exactly warm inside but it's shelter enough. Totally exhausted. He slumps on the floor. There are bags of compost and he sets them out on the floor and uses them as a mattress, and the shed's interior is barely big enough for his body but it will do. The air smells of soil. Which he finds soporific.

He dreams. But can't remember any of their content when he wakes up; or rather there are characters which he half-recognises but nothing violent enough occurs involving them to make the montage poignant. ... Marvin does, however, panic when he finds himself in this obscure box-like place and it takes him a minute to remember where he is and how he got here.

Right, I'm in this shed. A stranger's shed. He feels bad about breaking the door open. At the same time he's afraid there might be other folks about the area, so he opens the door very slightly. And peers out, to a cherubic morning with a wad of purple in the sky, *just* emerging from dawn. The house is dormant. Single house, big garden, affluent part of town – there are further rooftops down the street which he can see but they must be empty too ... all residents fled. Marvin shuts the door again. He drinks some water and he has one orange left in his bag and he eats that and the citrus magic blasts his mouth and he feels it slide into his stomach. As he chews he looks around the shed. There's a lot of useful stuff in here. Tools and rope and whatnot. Marvin investigates. There's a pocket knife on the desk, alongside a newspaper, which is dated six weeks previously and is open at the sports page. He can use the newspaper to make fires and the pocket knife is old fashioned and has a nice wooden handle and he can use it for many obvious reasons. He keeps them. And that coil of blue rope hanging from a nail on the wall: it just seems like it might come in handy. Can't predict yet but it could be crucial for something. So he puts it all in his bag.

Marvin has cash in his wallet. To compensate for robbing these items he leaves a pile of notes neatly on the desk. And he would write a note to say sorry about the door and the missing stuff, but he's not all that good with words and doesn't have a pen anyway, and he puts a hammer pressed down on the notes in case (he imagines) the breeze from the broken door might weave in and blow them all away. And he's basically doing it out of gesture. In the hope that whoever once lived here will find the money after all this doom is gone. *Cash is nothing*, he thinks as he looks at the pile, *but I can still hope*.

Okay. Let's start a new day.

He exits the shed and there's a bench nearby in the garden and Marvin pulls the bench up to the front of the door to stop it from bashing open in the wind, and then he climbs up over the fence again and jumps into the street.

Marvin walks.

He passes through this district and comes upon a weird square building with white walls and a funnel in its back yard and he gets closer and closer wondering what it is and the whole place is shut down and it has barbed wire fences around the perimeter which aids his curiosity. Marvin finds a sign, eventually, and it's a 'blood-bank'. *Hmm.* He's never seen a blood-bank before. This is what they look like apparently and he wonders why the building is so securitised and wonders what the blood containers look like inside the vaults or whatever … wonders what will happen to the collective blood now that we're in the aftermath.

On he goes and he's on this tight passage now with nice mounds of trees and ivy by it and he comes across this streetlamp which is blinking in a terrific vermillion, darker than that, this devilish colour and it could belong in the past century from which it was built and it sends these blinking spasms across the ivy leaves and Marvin stands there *wishing* that he was alive, here, the same age, 100 years back. Why has this one lamp been left alone, with its old technology, whilst all the others are an ugly white?

Anyway. That was the only lamplight still on in this weird street because it was surrounded by trees. All the others as he continues are off because the morning light picks up.

He gets to a new street and he passes a high school. Which literally looks like a prison. And is even more barricaded than that blood-bank was. … Marvin heads up a main street and he comes to this square with takeaway shops and a hairdresser and a chemist and all of them are unspoiled: all their shutters are down and they haven't been destroyed or robbed from. … Onto this crossroads. Where he finds a sign. And he knows the name of the district north of here. And that's fitting because it confirms he's going in the right direction.

Marvin's next route is a long one which passes by a train track, as in an overground one and the electrical wires tingle and prickle and he wonders whether the electricity's still running through them or whether it's just their gnarly aura making atmosphere.

He becomes aware of a darkening of the sky, as he passes by the tracks.

And initially he thinks it might be rainclouds, but the colour bespeaks of something else. Marvin comes to a car/railway crossing and there is a quartet of traffic pole lights (all of them deceased) which ogle him as he crosses the lines and then he moves down and he finds himself in new streets and realises where he is. He didn't think he'd gotten to this point.

The street below him stretches down in style and he has an impressive spanning image of the urbanity.

The stadium. Soccer stadium. The grassroots working class one. Marvin has no interest in soccer but he knows the football team because he knows the city and has seen the civilians wearing the strips/scarves and the sports news headlines and so on. So he knows of it and it confirms he's headed northernly at a productive rate. But there's something up with the stadium.

Indigo smoke plumes from it. It's either on fire or was on fire recently and this is the aftermath … There is the rectangle of the stadium and then these sooty clouds blooming from it … From this distance he can see no human involvement around it. No people. *Ehhhh, so what's up with this? This is the way I need to go but I shouldn't go near the stadium. What did they do? Did rival supporters arson the stadium or something? As in hooliganism or whatever it's called? It's amazing how stupid all that shit is.* There might be packs of young idiot men about. Marvin should make a detour.

From this vantage point, he can make out the flood control channel. Which underlies the traintracks and roads leading up to the stadium (and now he understands where that railway from before was leading).

Yes, the flood control channel leads in quite a convenient line up where he's headed. It's still quite close to the stadium but to the west of it, a quarter of a mile maybe. If Marvin moves fast he can get onto the flood channel and keep running from there.

That's the plan. Off Marvin sets. He goes down this long street and passes (yet more of) terrace housing and these ones have treacle walls and brown roofs and their chimneys are atavistic and he can imagine all the soccer fans back in the day walking down on the Saturdays and Sundays to the stadium with the flatcaps and so on before modernity and money killed off all of that romanticism.

Marvin takes a decisive left at the bottom of this passage, heading west.

There are scores of bottles on the streets. Un-smashed. Major parties must be happening. Marvin's afraid he might bump into the leftover attendees, that there might be goers going ... but he sees nobody and then he comes under the pass of the train line and there is this wild funk of piss and faeces and he ups his pace to get out from under the shadows and then he walks past a bunch of warehouses beyond that and there are a barrage of seagulls atop one of them and he's learned to hate that specific type of bird and he thinks *if they try and assault me I will just take out the gun and shoot them* even though Marvin's an animal lover. (The handgun nestles in his pocket. Pregnant.) But the gulls stay there. And he passes the warehouse park and he comes to the flood channel.

This brash stretch of amoral concrete, with berserk aslant walls either side, imposing.

There's a straggly gate leaning above one of said diagonal walls, which Marvin steps over and then he uses the grip of his boots to sidle down the surface. The concrete has this beige quality coupled with cracks and weather ware. And there are still tough weeds between the cracks and Marvin marvels at how they can sprout and survive in so barren a place. How the weeds even find a reason to pluck up in their spritely forms within a hostile realm.

A straight passage pulses before Marvin. It's not beautiful. But endearing. He travels.

There are small puddles around the area. Only pools. The little pockets of green weeds still amaze him and he thinks that when he was younger he didn't use to appreciate such insignificant things and Marvin questions whether his mind is turning and that he should try and not lose a hold of reality.

These overpasses come. The traintracks and roadbridges overhead and he walks under their tunnels. And whence inside he clucks his tongue. The echoes deal poppy tales around the tunnelwalls and his figure cuts and passes, as the resident novelist, and moves on.

The flood channel, as demented as it first seemed, becomes pleasant. Fond. It's this singular flow and the sky above it and nought else. And the tunnel-bits entice him. For when he can make those click echoes again.

Marvin's hasn't seen one of them (a tunnel) for a whiles and he's trekked a fair deal down the pass already. And he turns a bend in the channel. And ahead sees a tunnel in the far vision. And at the exact same instant he sees a person just before it.

A child.

By the small figure it must be a child. And yet it's an apparition ... Is it? This child just appears ahead of him and then it vanishes into the darkness of the tunnel. He can definitely see a person, a small body, walk down the regular path and then disappear under the tunnel. And it doesn't go beyond the other side.

"Is it real?" Marvin says to himself. He stays standing there watching for a time. Curious. Perhaps he is hallucinating? That image of the body was mercurial: maybe his imagination is off key.

He waits to see if anything will happen in the tunnel.

Nothing does and so he continues, placing it all down to his developing craziness.

ELISA

She drank the final can of soup last night and she's regretting it now.

Where else can she find food?

Elisa remembers this nightmare she had when she was younger. It was like being under an extractor fan, or right next to it, rather, and she could hear the whip-whop whip-whop of the blades in her face ... and all the whiles she was shackled to a bed. And this woman, who seemed like she was a nurse, or some kind of medical professional, was asking her a question. The same query, over and over. But she couldn't hear it because of the fan which kept going and the dream itself went on for an aeon, mindless, maddening. Nor did it have any climax or denouement. It was just a horrible desert, a long dose of pain.

Children remember dreams far better than adults.

Leaves fly about the street Elisa's currently on. They have nothing to do save be rushed around by the wind.

This dodgy scent has been in the air for some time and she's wondering what it is and as she continues the smell emboldens. *Burning? Is something burning?*

Elisa emerges onto a new street and she can see these rolling slabs of smoke in the sky. This isn't good. It comes from a structure she can't make out from where she is. So she walks down the street to the left to get a better view, wondering where the fire's from. And emerges around the corner. ... And, it's a soccer stadium. It's quite a while from where she is and it's no danger to her approximately ... *Why'd they burn the stadium? Was it all that idiot fan fighting stuff? Revenge because they hate each other? People still give a shit about football! In this situation?* Absurdity. Elisa continues west, sourcing another route and the land descends and she sees an overground railway. Which jars above her and she moves under its shadow. And then there is this unusual breakaway area beyond that which leads onto a fence and she goes up to that out of intrigue and looks down it.

It's a flood control channel.

If she can creep in through the fence this might be an easier passage than if she were to keep going through the streets, and it would keep her away from the burning stadium. So why not? ... She goes along the fence, which is a drab out-of-date affair, looking for a spot under the wire to slip through. And captures one quickly. Slips under the wire mesh and then she's on diagonal concrete. Which she slips down freely and playfully as if she were a videogame character, sliding on her shoes and backside and then she's at the bottom. She's in the flood channel now and it's stark and daunting but it might show results if she keeps going and there is no other option.

She walks.

(That nightmare, described above: she wonders what it means. And why it's returning now. If indeed dreams can ever *mean*, or be pinpointed for what their purpose is.)

Elisa trots and trots through this new situation and she turns this corner or wynd in the channel and then there's this tunnel ahead of her. With one of the tracks overhead and it's dark underneath. Spooky. And it kind of frightens her but she must go into it … And the vision in front of her is hard to confront and her senses are all poised on that …

Then she hears a noise *behind* her. Back down the channel.

There's a man. Just appearing around the curve. Advancing on her.

I have to hide. I'll hide in the tunnel. She skips away into the darkness of the tunnel.

There's a beam of steel running downside the wall. One of the rusty beams holding the bridge up; and it is fat enough to hide behind. She fits her frame into the nook behind the beam, and prays that this man won't see her in there.

There are countless thuggish seconds wherein she waits for this person to appear.

A tiny sliver of light from the end of the tunnel is there. And eventually this shape begins to wag shadows across it in larky shapes … Followed by footsteps. This man appears into her sight and she can't discern him that well and he's looking about the contours of the tunnel. Then he spots her. Pinned to the wall. They see each other. It's she that screeches first:

"I'm not an enemy! Leave me!"

Her voice makes him retract. He breathes and trembles and she looks up at him. And when he speaks in return his voice is mellow and pure. He says,

"I'm not an enemy either … I thought I saw somebody just before. Before I got in the tunnel I mean. I didn't know you were there …"

She blinks.

"I don't mean any harm whatsoever," he says, "I can help

54

you if you want? You look very young? I'll go on to the other side of the bridge ... and if you want some aid then you can come too. If not then you can stay there. I don't mind."

"Okay."

"Okay."

She watches him go and he walks on awkwardly. She watches him and he's a wellbuilt man and quite tall, about six feet, and he seems half and half of a combination of things she can't quite analyse. Half of that is surprise and the other half mystery and so she's intrigued. By him. She believes in him. And so she gets up and follows him out into the end of the tunnel, into the sunlight. ... He's actually already walked on, thinking that she hasn't come to meet him. And so she calls out:

"Hello," and then he turns back.

He has a bland, unmemorable face. Nor does said face express much when he says:

"Hello, there ..." and he stops.

Elisa stops too.

He looks down at her. Then he says,

"Are you cold?"

Then he takes his main coat off and lifts the jumper he has under that off and he steps towards her and gives it to her. "Take this," he says. And Elisa's bemused by the whole situation and doesn't know how to react. But the jumper is warm from his body heat. So she takes it and finds herself lifting off her own coat and then putting it on and obviously it's man size and it dwarfs her own torso. In a pleasant way.

"You're out here all on your own?" the man says.

"Yes."

The man thinks about asking where her parents are. If she has any. But he doesn't.

"How old are you?" he says.

"Eight."

"I can give you some food if you like ..." he says and he brings his bag out. (All this time Elisa keeps physically wary and distant from him, afraid he will do something to her.) "I have a can of spaghetti, in tomato sauce? You like spaghetti? I don't have a spoon. But it's still edible."

He leans across to her and gives her the can. Which she takes. "Thanks," she says. "Thank you so much." And she unpeels the cap and lifts the spaghetti into her mouth, trying not to seem as ravenous as she actually is, trying to be polite about it and not slurp. There is a satisfaction in feeding a child, for the man. He sits down the other side of the channel wall and he drinks some water. Then when Elisa has finished the spaghetti can he offers her the water bottle and she doesn't seem so coy of him anymore and she drinks from that too.

"Thanks for this," she says, "I really appreciate it."

"No worries at all. So where are you going?" he says to her.

"North."

"I'm going north as well … Can I help you?"

"What do you mean?"

"You can accompany me if you like? Even if it's just to the end of this channel."

She freezes. Elisa is unsure whether to trust this person; she's lost a lot of admiration for humanity in recent times. … But this man is unusual.

"I just don't want a kid out here alone, with all this mayhem going on. I can protect you. Until you get to where you want to get to."

"How can you protect me?"

"Ho. I honestly can. I promise."

"All right."

"All right? Good." He jerks on this feet for a bit, wondering how to form his next sentence. "I don't even know your name yet. What's your name?"

"Elisa."

"I'm Marvin."

Marvin offers a handshake and she shakes it and both of their fingers are clammy and it's vaguely goofy, but that slight tremulous embrace is the pitch of a bond.

ANTHONY BURTON

Anthony's mother Mandy had a far greater impact on his childhood than Cecil did. So she deserves her own chapter.

As mentioned hitherto, Mandy was much different from Cecil. The popular flashy extrovert versus the withdrawn husband; why did she marry him? What'd she ever see in him? ... Anthony was an indrawn kid too and yet he remembers being peppered with joy by Mandy. She was very close to him, when he was a toddler. And she used to take him around to her girlfriend's houses for lunch and he would play with their kids. When he was still cute. Then he got a bit older and he stopped being a tot and he was supposed 'to talk' to the ladyfriends ... and he couldn't. He didn't have a sparky tongue. Mandy was embarrassed of him. So she stopped taking him out. Altogether, actually, eventually. Mandy lost interest in him and he was left alone in the house a lot. Cecil was rarely there on weekends. Or if he was he was locked up in his study. Studying who knows what – he'd go into the room and not reappear until the night time. ... And this was in a suburb where everybody else along the street were in their forties and fifties and their kids were either in their late teens or had already gone off to college. So there was no social contact in a peer context. ... All Anthony had, was a piano in the living room. Cecil bought it originally and rarely ever got into playing it – although when he did play he already knew how, and was pretty good – another of his mysteries. Anthony taught himself the piano. The radio was on a lot in the kitchen and it played assorted music. He figured out the chords from what had gotten into his brain. And played around with them. Learned the chords with his right hand first and then with his left, and then he made melodies with his right fingers. The piano became a friend to him. Anthony thought he was getting adept with the instrument. Thought he was being creative.

Mandy would come home late. Almost every Friday and Saturday. Drunk. Cecil would go to bed early. And his bedroom was on the other side of the house from the living room, and so Anthony could keep playing the piano until late. And often he would be in there when Mandy returned. Mandy was a stunner. Even whence drunk. She didn't hold back with her looks and she had this chronic perfume whiff and she always kissed her boy when she saw him and the lips were always saucy but he liked it when a lipstick stain was left there and he didn't rub it away immediately. ... She was, simultaneously, a total wreck. Fried out of her brain. Alcohol obviously and cigarettes but probably a whole lot more. And Anthony smelled aftershave too, as in, the male's equivalent, and he knew that she hadn't been with Dad that night and this notion left this low feeling in his gut. ... Mandy's favourite fashion style/choice was skirts. She had great legs. A lot of her bust showed too. So she would return home on these nights whilst Anthony was at the piano and after the bubbly kiss would humph down on the sofa and she would ask him to play her something. Anthony knew some pop songs, simple ones – he was dead nervous and intent on pleasing her. She lay on the sofa with her skirt fluffed up over her thighs and sometimes he could see her panties. ... When children witness their parent drunk, it is such a deflated helpless uneasy feeling. A loss of control which they cannot overtake. Mandy listened. Anthony *thought* she was listening. And she'd grin at the end and clap and cheer. ... And so he did start to believe he had some talent with the piano. ... Would practice extra hard for her late arrivals on these nights, learn new bits, and look forward to her asking him to play again. And indeed, there came the famous night. Summer. Dandy, still warm at night; Cecil was asleep, Mandy came home carousing ... and this time she didn't kiss him, only passed him in the living room and went into the kitchen and got another drink (gin, with ice cubes) and then sat on the couch. "Play, then," she said.

Her frostiness toppled him and he tried to play what he'd prepared but he couldn't do it well and it came out clunky and nervous and tame.

He stopped early. And she *smirked*. Anthony looked at her searchingly. The makeup on her face was all a-drizzle. Streaks down the cheeks, from the eyelashes: she'd been crying. But she wasn't now. And yet her eyes were still shining with the breath of cruelty. When she said:

"What are you playing the piano for, Anthony?"

"Just because I like it."

"But why are you playing with it? On it?"

"It's fun."

"What do you want to *do* with it though?"

"I don't know ..."

"You want to be a great pianist one day?"

" ... "

"Why don't you answer?"

"I do not know what you mean."

"Do you think you will be a great man one day?"

And then she glugged her drink down after that whilst her boy still sat on the piano stool. He never responded.

"You'll need to do better than that in life, son," she said, "if you don't even have a word for this. If you don't want to be a great man, then what else do you want to focus on? What's the point in being alive? You need to connect with people. Help people. Have an influence on other folks, even if it's a menial thing you do. If not, why were you even born?"

She stood up and her skirt went down her thighs and she looked as if she might collapse and in this moment she was suddenly ugly and old.

"Hmm?" she said. "Hmm!"

When he didn't answer she stomped out of the room and upstairs with her glass.

Anthony Burton's thinking about all of this, in the present, on a clean motorway.

These incidents, memories, happened around fifty years ago. He thought he'd banished bits like this, left them in the past. As he drives, along the monotonous stretch, he revisits the scenes. Glamourous and cinematic they are. He wishes the memories would stop. Or at least ease. Ultimately wishes they would leave him be.

RUBY-ROSE

There's blood on her coat. She's been aware of it for some time, but hasn't had the guts to stop cycling, just to get as far away as possible, concentrating on the pedals. She can't stop shuddering. But she comes to the bottom of a hillside and doesn't think she can get up it without cleaning these stains off. *His* stains. So she stops her bike and sets it by a hedge.

On the pavement there lie puddles. She has tissues in her pockets and she wets them in the pools and then rubs at her coat with the water. Which luckily has the right fabric to cleanse well. Then she notices there's some (blood) on the collar of her shirt and she takes it off feverishly and scrubs at it with the moisture. The sight scares her. She rubs too hard and the tissues fall apart. Ruby-Rose weeps. The tears splash on her murderous hands. She's wasting too many of her tissues and the shirt is not getting any cleaner. So she scrunches it up. There's a bin by a bus stop nearby her and she chucks it inside that. There's another shirt in her bag and so she puts that on instead. Then gets on her bike and cycles up the hill. ... Which takes some while. It's quite a high-brow area of the town. Lots of pine woodland and big single houses with rangy driveways. Hypnotic green of the pine needles and gaudy scent of the sap and the flurrying of the squirrels. Houses look unscathed by the looting, albeit she is some distance from the city centre by now. Their garden flowers are mostly dead, and the lawns covered with the leaves from the fancy trees. ... For miles there is no movement save from the squirrels and birds, until at length she sees a vehicle approaching her, a blip on the other hillside. She would rather avoid it and so she takes her bike off the road and up over the railings by the hill and hides it and herself in the gorse bushes and she lies there amid the scratchy brush. Anticipating this vehicle. *What if they see me here? And get out and confront me and find out what I did? What if it's the police themselves? What if there's still blood on my clothes and they see it and will find out what I am?* And the rushing sound of the vehicle makes this drawn-out entrance with rolling echoes across the hillside and she just has to stay there as it nears and then it erupts above her and passes on and then there is an equally superb diminuendo. ... Ruby-Rose remains there in the bushes. It feels (undeservedly) pleasant to relax, and though it's windy it's still not overtly cold. And under the branches and through the grass on the floor she can see ants going about their business. Tiny courageous creatures. Ants ants ants, they whittle about the soil hills intricately. They don't even notice she's there. This giant human above them. She's getting sleepy, but she can't sleep here, so she gets up and pulls her bike back up onto the road and rides on.

The pines fall away. Leveller land arrives and it makes for smooth pedalling. She passes a golf course. She can see the flagpoles with their small flags a-flapping ... and the grass is unmown for however many weeks (six or seven?) and one wouldn't be able to play golf there. Not that she knows anything about the sport.

And then it gets dark. *Does* get chilly.

She has bike lights and she turns them on even though they'll probably be of no importance. As in, there won't be cars around to hit her. Avoid hitting her. But the street lighting here is poor and she's still in this leafy posh area and she slows her pace a bit because she doesn't want to crash. ... Then the night seems to *drop* and the temperature dip at the same time and its ferociously black and she's proper nervous now. And she's fixated on the track in front of her, worried ... and then, boom, she hears this pop behind her. Then her back wheel starts juddering. ... "Is it a flat? No way!" She stops and gets off and surveys the tyre. Yep, it's been flattened. It's still leaking air and it she watches it depress. ... Ruby-Rose wheels the tire to see what might've punctured it. And quickly finds this small *nail* which has done this so, quite perfectly. She pulls it out. An inch nail. Of all the luck, to drive on top of it in this obscure place.

Ruby-Rose does have a spare inner tube in her bag and she's fixed punctured tyres many many times in the past. And she gets the tube and the pump and so out of her bag now and she gets under the nearest lamplight to deal with it. ... But she's suddenly so jaded. It's night. The trail was already feeling hazardous. *Why not rest for now and fix the bike up in the morning?* ... She puts the stuff back in the bag and then looks around for somewhere to sleep. Obviously there's nowhere hospitable nearby. But she can't stay near the road. And over the nearest fence there's what looks like a park, i.e., (what use to be) a public park ... and actually there's a gate leading down to it, which she finds. She goes through that and down the path and the wind is left overhead and the atmosphere gets dreamy and she comes to this wide silky surface she spots in the distance and she realises it's a lake. Or a big pond rather. And this is where folks would come to dogwalk or eat picnics by the water and so on. She tugs the bike along. And finds one of those wooden open-shelter-hut things (whatever they're called) by the pond-side, where folks could take their picnics into if it were raining. ... This suits for a shelter. She can camp here for tonight. The hut has a bench which she can lie on. Won't be comfy but she has her sleeping bag. She unties that from her rucksack and lays it out on the bench and then slips inside it and she lies there, using her hands for a pillow ... There are intricate sounds from the lake. These infinitesimal sloshing whispers. As if it were alive. Despite the volume being at fairy levels, it keeps her from sleeping. *And yet, why should I sleep? How can I ever be allowed to sleep again?*

It's odd being with a child. Walking with her. She's a fragile thing; he looks down at her trying to think up things to say: she knows he's looking at him and keeps her own face downward. It's not exactly the scenario for idle conversation.

Across the arch of the flood channel come a flock of starlings – seemingly out of nothing – and they make this collective flushing noise like a calm wave on a shoreline and they fly in tremendous tandem and Marvin and Elisa watch them with the same awe. In a skilful black brushstroke they do this pirouette on the ivory sky and then they vanish just as nonchalantly.

"Amazing birds," Marvin says …

"Yeah, they are."

On they walk.

"How long have you been on the road, Elisa?" Marvin ventures.

"I've lost count of all the days."

"Okay … Which district of the city are you from? Were you from, before the Crash?"

She tells him. His eyes widen. Because that's pretty much the other side of the metropolis.

"Wow! And you came all this way by yourself?"

Elisa nods.

Her shoes are muddy and worn and pixielike. She has these sharp eyes with razor eyelashes and they never quite stall on any one thing. Elisa's thinking. He can't tell what she's thinking about. There's a moment of quiet. Which *she* then breaks:

"Did you see much of the riots?"

"Some of them, yes. I was lucky enough to get out quickly. I lost my flat, but I'm still lucky enough. … Yourself?"

"Yes I saw a lot of it … First hand. It was terrifying, wasn't it?" Nor does Elisa look at him as she speaks.

"Of course it was."

"But I think the rioting will phase away," Marvin goes, "I think they will all tire out. It can't last forever."

"Maybe. I don't think this city will ever be the same again though," she says.

And he wants to say something consoling in response to that, but the verbal ammunition never comes.

They get to the end of the flood channel and discover new streets. Lots of old flats, these sallow jutting gaunt cuboids with empty carparks. … The traintrack too which the flood channel meets and underpass below that and they go up these steps into this new hood and there is a train station close by. They approach the station to check the sign to see where they are. (There's a map outside of the station doors.) Good news. They're more than on track. A decent chunk of northernly travel.

It's mid afternoon by now. There's a bench nearby on the street.

"Do you want to take a break for now, Elisa?" nodding towards the bench. "Fancy a snack?"

"Yes, okay …"

They go over to the bench and she sits the far end of him.

Marvin's 29. Elisa's 8. They don't know each other. Marvin gives her a bar of cheap supermarket milk chocolate, whilst he's unwrapping his own bar himself.

Elisa watches him. He has watery irises and waify eyebrows and nondescript hair too, short. There's nothing remarkable about his appearance and yet he still surprises her.

She bites into some of the chocolate and this explosion of cocoa goes through her head and the sugar is immense – only one block of it and it swarms down her throat. She chokes a little bit. Mildly. Marvin laughs and he hands her the water bottle. She drinks from it. Screws the cap back on and hands it back.

"I don't understand," she says to him.

"Don't understand what?"

"Why you are being kind?"

"Well … why not …"

"It's just surprising. Is all."

"Me being kind?"

"Yeah."

"I'm not being overly nice, kiddo. It's no major rescue. We're in the same situation. Both headed the same place. … I'm not that likeable a man, but I can support you until we get there."

"Well, thank you …"

Marvin winks at her.

ELISA

They walk until it gets to night and the wind pushes them and the wind changes the clouds in the sky too and it gets cold enough for them to suck into their clothes as far as they can.

(Through the spaces in the clouds appear these marvellous rainbow spots of stars which prickle and pierce. There's Orion and Cassiopeia … but her favourite constellation is the 'Seven Sisters' ((The Pleiades)) – that dainty clique of cosmic magic.)

The neighbourhood they're in is a bit imposing. Those flatblocks keep replicating and they're filled up with low housing under them and Marvin's half-sure they're headed the correct way but they've been walking for quite some time and Elisa is obviously cold and she can't go as fast as he can and she hasn't the same levels of stamina. … Marvin wishes he could find somewhere for them to rest. But this district shows no signs of relenting. Moreover – the place is disconcerting. Empty bottles and smashed bottles. A whole load of further detritus across the floor as if a long cheap party's just died.

But then there's a noise. Elisa is the one that hears it first.

"Marvin," she whispers, "I think I hear something. People, up ahead."

"I think I hear folk too, Elisa. But don't fret."

The sounds are of shouting and cooing, idiot noises. Male. Virile.

"We should run, Marvin," Elisa says, louder this time. "I don't want to see these men."

"Elisa, don't worry."

"They'll hurt us."

"They can't. Hurt us."

The noises of the men increase.

There's a side street just to the right of Elisa. And she grabs Marvin's arm and tries to pull him along and she's almost teary, she can feel her ducts brace, trying not to cry … Marvin puts an arm around her back and brings her on.

And simultaneously this group of males appear at the end of the street. Just as she fears.

Four of them. They're kicking a football about between them and they're drunk and probably high too on whatever else. … Either party are maybe fifty yards apart. One of the lads boots the football awry and it bundles down the road … and they all go "wayyyyy" because he did a silly kick. And it's only then that they see Marvin and Elisa down the road. And all of them hush upon the sighting, the funny mood snuffed out.

"Please, Marvin," Elisa pleads, "let's run."

"Trust me, Elisa. Be easy."

The men have stopped moving entirely. Apart from the one that's collecting the football from the road, which he picks up and holds against his chest. They go mute. And stay that way as Marvin brings Elisa up the passage.

The one holding the football comes towards them.

He wears this orange hooded top with a conglomerate sports brand across the chest and he's quite a handsome man and broadchested; he has tall cheek bones and raunchy hair: and he has a swagger in his step.

His three cronies aren't as pretty physically but they're of the same ilk clothes wise … and age wise. Must be nineteen, twenty, that kinda age. All apocalyptic and keen on carnage. The trio stand behind and watch curiously as orange-hoody man confronts Marvin and Elisa.

"How you chaps doing?" he says.

"Not bad, man," Marvin goes, "Yourself?"

"I'm pretty good. … What you doing out here?"

"Just walking."

"Walking where?"

"On our way out of here. Just passing by."

"Hmm, right …" the man looks at Elisa, and says, "is that your daughter?"

"So what if she is?"

"Don't get cheeky with me, boyo. I asked if she is your daughter."

"No, she's not."

"Then what are you with her for?"

"We're friends."

"Hmm … I don't believe you," and then the man addresses Elisa directly and he says to her, "Is this man your friend?"

And she says,

"Yes, he is."

The answer annoys the man.

He looks around to his cronies and their feet and fists are prickling.

"What you got in those bags there?" the orange goon says. "They look heavy. What's in them?"

"Only our items," Marvin says, "and we'd appreciate it if you would just leave us be and let us walk by."

Orange goon smirks and he's full of bravado. The other lads begin to edge towards the scene and their eyes are boyish and greedy.

"I just want to see what's in those bags? You know that people are starving, right?" the man says to Marvin.

"I do yes, but this is our stuff and we intend to keep it."

"You don't want to share?"

"I share with my friends."

"Am I not your friend?"

"You don't seem like it."

"That's very rude."

Amidst the dialogue the three other lads have come a lot closer and the two parties are in a deadlock now.

"Will you just let us go on, please?" Marvin says.

Orange man drops the football he's holding. He traps it under his foot. And then brings something else out from his back pocket.

Which is a switchblade. And he presses the button and it pings open. This thin dark blade pops erectile.

"I wanna see what's in your bags, brother and sister," he says, and he points the knife at them.

...

Marvin wonders what type of varmint scum he's really dealing with here. He knows that there is this unprecedented situation with the Crash and the giant loss of money, and that, yes, people are going hungry, but: to try and rob this man and this little girl? That's crazy and beyond acceptability. That's beyond anything.

Are most people morally lazy or do they just turn to madness after an overload of strife? After passing the limit to how much they can take? ... Marvin has been affected the Crash. It's made him homeless. He's had to leave his home. Serious as that. Then he finds this girl on the streets. He wants to help her. This idiot band of lads find her and instead would quite happily steal from her.

"Come on, son," orange man says to Marvin. Pacing closer with the blade.

"Stop there, man."

"Why should I stop?"

"Just do it."

And his cronies are descending on the team too, intent on

violent fantasy.

Marvin reaches into his inner jacket pocket.

And takes out his handgun.

He clutches the handle hard and wields it swiftly and aims it upon orange man's forehead.

Which licks a perfect silence across the arena and everybody stops moving.

Marvin aims it right in this handsome man's face. And his three cronies see the gun. And they panic – and they just run away. They abandon him and bail, sprint off down the street. Orange man looks around and watches them, watches their cowardly deed unfolding, and there is this expression of complete surprise in his face. Surprise, that his brothers are actively betraying him. He turns back, and stays there, distilled, watching this weapon's nozzle trained on his nose.

"I asked you to leave us alone," Marvin says to him.

"I'm sorry. I'm sorry." Orange man says, shrivelled now, defeated.

Marvin waits until all of his mates have abandoned him at the end of the street.

And then he lowers the gun and points it onto the road just in front of Orange man's feet, and fires twice. Lumps of concrete spit up as the bullets bash.

Elisa covers her ears. Claps her hands to her eardrums with the berserk volume. Orange man shrieks and jumps back. Fantastic thundery echoes whirl around the mass arena.

And then he turns and bolts.

He runs after his comrades who just deserted him. (Leaving the football behind too.)

Elisa's ears sing from the blasts.

Marvin puts the handgun back in his inside pocket. He admits that he feels powerful but the dominant emotion is one of relief. That it worked. The gun, as a deterrent.

Elisa looks up at him and his entire frame is shivering as if he were shaking from a bad dream. He bends down to her and asks her if she's okay. And she hugs him.

She does it instinctively and he clutches her back. She doesn't even know why she does it; it just happens.

"We have to keep going now a bit longer," he says, "all right?"

Elisa nods. It's hard to hear his voice.

"So if we go fast for one last burst and get away from this

neighbourhood, then we can sort out a place to sleep. Can you do that?"

"I can, yeah."

"Good. Let's go."

ANTHONY BURTON

A stretch of blue sky opens above the motorway. This single bar of blue amidst the clouds, and then it grows, like spilled dye, and then the sun emerges for a period and its shine enriches everything.

It cheers Anthony. He pulls in to a stop lane and parks. And lights his pipe. There are thick bushes by the lane and this gnarly field and he can hear the birds and there's a rabbit too he spots from afar, bubbling about with a white tail. Then it vanishes in the shrubbery and doesn't come back. ... He finishes his pipe. And he should keep driving with this open way of road but he could also just do one more bowl, with the nice sunny brightness through the windscreen (even if a lot of it is cracked). Why not? So he loads it up and puffs onwards. And looks ahead, eyes wandering.

There's a left entrance which conjoins with the main motorway, 100 metres yonder. And Anthony doesn't notice it instantly, but this person appears there. Walking, out of the entrance and then he (it's a male from what he can see from here) takes up a route on the grass by the road. And keeps going. It's a civilian, and he looks young. Anthony's curious. The civilian hasn't peered back yet and spotted Anthony's van sitting there. *What's this lad doing out here in this desolation? Perhaps I could approach him – offer him a lift? Rather than him having to walk all this way.* He smokes the last of the bowl down and then blows the embers out of the window and starts the van up and heads down to meet this character, at a far slower pace than the motorway speed limit.

The boy hears the van. His body and face snap around, afraid. Anthony feels bad for frightening him and in order to seem less imposing he toots his horn at the boy in a soft double patter, to try and seem like he's not meaning any harm. And the lad stays there on the grassy mound, watching. ... Indeed, he's very young. Must be a teenager. He wears a hoody and jeans and a hiking bag and tough boots. Has straggly beginnings of facial hair, not quite there yet. Anthony waves to him and then he pauses the van and rolls his left window down and calls out to the boy.

"Hello there, son. You all good?"

"Yeah, I'm fine."

"Where you headed?"

"Just down the pass … I'm fine."

"Yes but where about?"

"On the way to Newton Mound."

"Newton Mound?"

(Anthony has seen the name of the town several times on the roadsigns that he's passed and the last one if he remembers correctly said it was 8 miles off. He can easily do the boy a favour.)

"Yeah."

"Okay, well I'm on my way there anyway. In the same direction I mean. So I can give you a lift if you like?"

"… Thanks for the offer, but really it's no bother."

"Honestly, it'll save you a long walk. I'm literally going that way anyway. And there's room in the van if you wanna come along too."

The boy looks up and he spots the damage on the windscreen. Then darts his eyes back to Anthony.

"It wasn't me that did that, son," Anthony chuckles, "I'm not going to beg you to take the lift. The offer's there if you want it."

"Right. Okay, thank you."

The boy comes off the grass and towards the van and gets in through the left door and he shuts it and sits on the seat farthest from Anthony (there being three seats in the front). Anthony takes off. The lad coughs a little from the pipesmoke still in the van.

"So what's your story, son?" Anthony says.

"I don't really have one?"

"Are you in trouble? You shouldn't really be out on your own in times like these."

"Nah I'm not in trouble. I'm one of the fortunate ones."

"How do you mean?"

"My folks weren't affected by the Crash. Neither was our town much. We were just fortunate is all."

"So you stay with your folks?"

"Yeah."

"Good. I'm glad. But why are you so far away from home?"

"What do you mean?"

"If your folks are in Newton Mound why do I find you on the motorway 8 miles away from it? You just out hiking?"

"Ho, no, I don't live in Newton Mound: I'm just going to visit a friend there. I used to take the bus to his town but obviously the buses aren't running now. So I just walk."

"I see, I see."

"I really appreciate the lift."

"No problem."

"So what happened to your windscreen."

"Ha. Kids. A bunch of cruel kids. Nothing too serious."

The boy looks up at him for an extended answer, but he's not going to get it, so he never asks any further. And there's a balance of mutual quietness. And in not too long they pass another roadsign which says: Newton Mound – 6 m.

"What about you?" the lad goes, "Where are you headed? You escaping the city?"

"I suppose I'm neither lucky or unlucky. Shouldn't complain considering what's happened to some. To many. Yes I need to leave town for a while. Hopefully I can return. One day. Maybe not. I'm mad with the world but I'm still alive."

"Do you think that it'll get better?"

"The whole situation you mean?"

"Yeah."

"I don't know, kid. It could do. Will take time though. The city will need a lot of repairing."

"Did it all kick off where you stayed?"

"Not *directly* no … But I'm too old. If my place got attacked they wouldn't have had any trouble with a fogey like me. … Anyway. What's your name, son?"

"Douglas."

"Nice to meet you Douglas, I'm Anthony Burton." As they're driving the sky changes again and this big bulk of cloud moves over the sun and in turn deals this gigantic shadow across the highway and then the van goes into the shadow and the shade dims the interior. "It's nice that you still have the confidence to go and see your friend in Newton Mound, Douglas. That you're trying to be normal, hanging out with friends. But I would be a bit more wary. Not every van driver who meets you will be like me. You understand?"

"Sure, sure. I get you."

They get to within 2 miles of Newton Mound and then they're pretty much there and Douglas says it's okay to just let him off on the grass again and he can walk down from there. The boy offers a parting handshake. He's trying to be manly when he does it and he's a bit awkward but Anthony gets that he's trying hard. … Anthony drives on and leaves his figure in the reflections of the side mirrors. ... He pities the lad for being so young. Being about 30 years younger than him; and thus thirty extra years, for Douglas, witnessing what could unravel in the future world. It's already bad; most likely it'll get worse. Anthony's old. He will die, naturally, far sooner, whereas this kid will be around for the possible climax, the end. ... ... And then of course Anthony realises he's channelling what his own father used to say to him when he was a boy. As he read those newspapers. That gloomy line he always said. And he's ashamed with himself for regurgitating that mentality. ... *Perhaps I'm wrong. And perhaps that Douglas boy was right in hoping that it could get better soon. Maybe most people will prevail and overcome. I can be one of them. That child can as well.*

RUBY-ROSE

She wakes up to the squawk of a bird, and shoots up from the bench and her wits wildly gather together. That bird flies over the pond. She's cold but the sight of the pond is astounding. Much wider than it seemed in the dark last night and there's sun out too and the light radiates the surface, teeming and mystic. ... Ruby-Rose eats one of her rolls in her bag. Her bike's sitting there too with the duff back tyre ... she assembles the new tubing and the pump and after she's done eating gets to work on it. As she's pulling the rubber of the wheel down the back, her finger knicks something on the steel frame and she swears and brings her hand away and her pinkie is now bleeding and the blood dribbling down her forehand. She holds tissues to the cut. Then inspects the wheel to see what cut her. Ah. There's a tiny spiky bit of the metal on the upside of the framing. Hasn't noticed it before. Takes quite a while for the cut to stop bleeding. Goes into her bag for her toiletry bag which has plasters in it. Sticks two plasters back on it. As she's putting the plaster box back she notices the zippy upper pouch in her bag and she unzips it and checks that her precious things are still there. She brings the gem stone out. The one Emma gave her as a best friend gift when they were girls – emerald, magic. *What would Emma think of me if she were to know what happened yesterday? What I did? What will anyone ever think of me about that? Even if I ever get out of this madness.* She puts the stone back. Then returns to the tyre and avoids the little spike. And takes a swig of water and saddles the bicycle and rides onwards.

The park has a concrete path which is easy to cycle along. And in short time it leads back up to the road where she was before. She can see for a good few miles and at least has this certainty of direction and so she heads on.

Yes, holding that stone has now brought back memories of Emma. That sheltered materialistic childhood she shared with that girl; raised in big houses, going to a private school ... Ruby-Rose even had a nanny. She's 19 and she's never even had a job before: never needed to have one because of the parental wealth. Finished high school, went travelling for a summer and then got into this *prestigious* university at 18 and now she's out here on a hilly highway, barely knowing what she's doing. She killed a man yesterday. ... Her neck still smarts a bit from the attack and she whacked her elbow during the struggle too and that's aching a lot. But, she murdered him. Surreal. ... *I should never have left my apartment. Got too scared too quickly and left when I didn't need to. I'm too naïve. I'll never be the same again now.* ... The fact is that she cannot turn back now. The mistake is already done. And, who knows? Perhaps the looters did actually get to her flatblock and break in and trash the interior. If she were to return, even if she knew the way, it could be worse. She can't know for sure. ... Ruby-Rose is still in a leafy area with very few houses. Gratefully the roads are mostly downhill and she makes them in smooth time and the breeze toys with her hair. ... During one descent she notices something lying on the road. This little bobble of something she can't make out until she's close. A hedgehog. A squashed one. It's been there for some time – the flies have left it alone, been and gone. *Poor little chap.* She ponders whether to move it off the road as it seems disrespectful for a dead thing to just be left there to decompose. But she probably shouldn't touch it. *I hope you get reincarnated in a good way. Become something else. Have another life.*

MARVIN

They walk through the rest of the angry neighbourhood fast. The towerblocks fall away. The streets are mucky and frightening but they don't see another person after those four goons.

With panic they have hurried. And they've spent themselves physically and as soon as they're out of the town they feel it. Elisa especially. She lags. Her knees feel as if they might shatter. … Marvin and she come to a bridge, which is over a river, which they saw glimpses of within the town. The river's quite a long way down (enough to probably die on the impact if one were inclined to jump) and by the river's valley are thin strips of woodland. Save for the lamps on the bridge it's very dark and only getting colder and up here especially it's windy.

"Elisa," he says to her, half way along the bridge, "why don't we camp in the woods down in the valley overnight? I can make a fire. I'll give you my coat. We need to get some rest from the cold. Nobody should find us or see or smell the fire. You want to do that?"

"Yes let's try it."

Her voice is faint and she moves like a waif and they get to the end of the bridge and there's a wired fence by the roads leading into the woods and Marvin climbs over it and the fence is about as tall as Elisa is and Marvin asks her if it's okay to touch her and lift her over it and she says yes please and then he picks her up and does so and it surprises him how light weighted her body is … he goes into the pull thinking she would be heavier. … Their shoes crackle on the fallen leaves. They make their way down the valley, Marvin looking for a place in which to shelter, where the ground is flat enough to lie on for a while, even if it's for a few hours or until dawn comes. Marvin adopts his lighter from his back pocket. And rips it on. Elisa watches the flame make these orange black shadows around the tree limbs and she imagines that she could be living centuries back, could be in a book, that she's not real in the now … that Marvin is somebody else as well, a ghost, apparition: the fire has such the hypnotic zeal. They come to a group of holly bushes. And a small spot in the middle of them; dry leaves on the floor and circled by the evergreen of the holly. "This should do for a spot, Elisa," Marvin says. "Take a seat." She flops down. And this giant wave of fatigue hits her. "I'm gonna go looking for firewood, Elisa. It shouldn't take long. And then we'll get a fire going. For now, you want something to eat?" Marvin undoes his bag and looks inside. Out of the rations he wonders what to offer her. He rustles about idiotically and at one point he brings out these bags of crisps he has. (Ready Salted. Classic.) – "Those are fine," Elisa says, "please." – "The crisps?" – "Yes those are perfect." He hands her them. Then leaves for the firewood. She opens the bags and stuffs the crisps into her mouth. And there's nothing nutritious about the food and it's all factory potato and synthetic seasoning; but the salt gives her a rush and she chomps both bags down and the calories enter her body. And then Marvin comes back with a bundle of firewood. ... He sets it down on the ground and then begins preparing it. He's skilful; she watches him. "How'd you know how to do that?" she asks. – "Do what?" he says. "Build fires." – "Oh, just from practise. It's not that difficult." He lays a mesh of birch twigs down first and he lights that up with the flame and holds them together softly until the twigs befriend the heat and then he adds the larger sticks to it and the lofty grand scent of woodsmoke Elisa doesn't know so well and it's all new to her. Within five minutes there's a proper fire going and she sits closer to it. ... Marvin's hungry himself but he knows that he should probably save what food they have until they find further options. So he can forego for tonight. Besides, the heat from the fire's swell. Elisa's pupils are pinpointed by the glow of it. Marvin still knows almost nothing about her history, where her parents are, why she's out here. ... At the same time Elisa gets that he's watching her curiously. She's intrigued by him as well. Ever since the incident earlier in the night she's wanted to know why he owns a gun. Who is he? He's quite hard to compare to other people. Doesn't have much of an accent, rarely ever talks, is dressed quite efficiently, is helping her out and she knows his first name and is learning his face and physique. But who is Marvin, really? ... As she sits by the fire she's immersed in the burning gold of the embers. And she looks up at him. Both of them look at each other at the same time. Elisa was just about to ask him that sentence, "Why do you have a gun?" and then she hesitates. Then Marvin says, "So I'll give you my coat. So you can have a cover." And he stands up and takes his coat off. ... And obviously his handgun is still there, in the coat, and he takes it out and lays it on the floor, and Elisa sees it again and it's as if Marvin is embarrassed by its presence. Marvin gives her his coat and she drapes it around herself. She's muffled by the weight and security of it. – "But what about you?" Elisa says. "Won't you be too cold?" – "Nah, kiddo, I'll be good, I'll keep the fire going. … Just lie down and rest now. We'll get up when it gets light. Okay?" – "Okay. Thanks Marvin." … Elisa lies on the leaves and she smells the cold soil under them and she lifts Marvin's jacket hood up over her face and she can smell him as well – a whole mixture of another body. And she listens to the snaps and pops of the fire and she's far too exhausted to enter dreamland but she heads into sleep, a form of it … an island of distant slumber.

ELISA

There's a stinging in her throat when she swallows. First thing she notices when she wakes. She hopes it's because she's just risen … but it persists. That clamping sharp pain around the tonsils. *Oh no. Am I getting ill? I can't be sick out here.* She lifts Marvin's hood from her face and it's still quite dark and the fire has gone down and has shy light now and Marvin's asleep the other side of it, lying on his side. At least he's with her. She puts some more of the firewood on the embers and it lifts up gradually and she lies back down and watches the shapes and coils in the tiny inferno. And tries to convince herself that her tonsils aren't sore. And pulls the hood back over the eyes and manages to get back to sleep.

She has a dream. That she's back at home and she's in her bed. But she can't sleep. Because there's this odd noise coming from down the hallway. It's this peculiar intermittent knocking sound, as of wood being tapped or clopped together. Comes from the kitchen. She gets out of bed and opens the door. And listens. The house is dark, with no light in the corridor or the kitchen. … She walks down the hallway and gets to the kitchen door and peers inside. Her mother's standing over the cooker with her dressing gown on and her back bent down at a pot. There is an ounce of light from outside the kitchen window which is the only way Elisa can see her. … The pot has no gas on. But her mother stirs at it with a wooden spoon. Then she stops at that. And goes to a chopping board which is by the cooker. Picks up a fat knife. And begins making these chops at the wood. And she holds onto something with her left hand, as if her fingers were clasped around something. But there's nothing there. No vegetables, or items at all on the board. The knife just taps and taps at nought. Elisa stands there in the doorway. What can she do about this? She's hesitant to go nearer to her mother … and yet she's that close. … Mother stops chopping and puts the knife down and she picks up an imaginary handful of items and places them in the pot and then she stirs it. Her hand pauses. And she turns around. And sees Elisa behind her. And she screams. Her pitch is shrill, horrible, villainess. Elisa cries out, "I'm sorry, Mum" and she switches the kitchen lightswitch on. And her mother turns fully around and there's something injured about her body and the image is only there for a second because Elisa feints with shock …

And then she wakes up.

With a small gasp. She's in the woods again. Then when she sits up, Marvin's looking at her. He's by the fire and it's very early morning.

"Did you have a bad dream?" he says.

"Yes …"

"Oh no, well. It's over now. You can relax."

Dusk. A handful of birds sing in the trees and their melodies are lovely but the noises hurt her head. Plus, her whole mouth stings from the tonsils yonder and her head feels like lead.

"You okay?" Marvin says.

"Yeah," she lies. "But can I sleep a bit longer?"

"Of course. You don't need to ask. We can head on when it's full morning."

She does get a bit more rest in. But every time she swallows her saliva gets caught and these dots tickle her throat and won't go away. Elisa doesn't dream again, or quite sleep. Marvin is very quiet by the fire and it's as if he's not even there. She wishes she doesn't have to address the new day … but the light enhances under the hood and she can see the myriad wondrous colours of the leaves by her eyes. Eventually she just has to get up.

Expecting to see Marvin there. But he's gone. Not there. Spasm of panic. *Did he leave me? Did Marvin leave!* She looks down and his rucksack is still there. But she's still worried because she can't see him anywhere.

"Marvin," she calls out to the trees, "Marvin? Where did you go?"

About thirty seconds pump by and she's just about to call out to him again but then there's a rustling in the bushes and he appears, also looking concerned.

"What's up, Elisa?"

"Oh … there you are."

"Something wrong?"

"No. I just. Thought you might have left."

"Ho. No – I was just down at the river. Just went down for a look at the river."

Marvin comes over to her. And he gets to his rucksack and brings out a flapjack bar. And hands it to her.

"You familiar with flapjacks, Elisa?" he says.

"Not that much."

"Well – you haven't lived then. Here you go. It's a good

thing to have as breakfast."

She thanks him and she unwraps the packet and takes a bite of it and the sugar and cream and oats go into her mouth and the combination is delicious. To her tastebuds. Until she gulps. And this ripe pain whacks her throat and it's hard not to wince. And she doesn't want to seem ungrateful to Marvin for giving her the food. … She looks up to him to see if he's watching her. But he isn't. He's moving stuff around inside his bag.

(Marvin has black hair with swishes of grey in it and a thin nose and unusual jaw. His face is quite often expressionless and his voice is nearly always monotone – she hasn't yet heard him speak loudly or with much inflection. Even with that gun incident with the goons. He spoke calmly with the same tonality, before and after the shooting.)

Elisa feels the bite of flapjack sink into her stomach.

She doesn't think she can take another bite because of that agony.

"I really like the flapjack," she says to Marvin, "but I don't have an appetite."

"Okay."

"So I can save the rest for later? Or, you want to eat it?"

"Save it for later, by all means."

"Cool."

"Shall we move on now then."

"Yeah."

She gives him back his coat. She puts her bag on.

"What about the fire?" she asks.

"We can just leave it be … We don't have to put it out. It's cold and it will pass away soon."

"Shame. It was a nice one."

Marvin notices that her balance is a bit off-key. As she stands. That her eyelids are still drowsy.

"You sure you're all right, Elisa? You seem a bit woozy …"

Elisa thinks *maybe I should tell him that I think I've caught some kind of illness. Flu, fever.* But she's still in denial, and thus she lies, again:

"I am … Uh hu. Only a bit tired. Let's get moving."

Marvin's unconvinced. But they have to leave these woods either way. And so he leads the way out of them, back up the valley.

ANTHONY BURTON

He comes upon a sign which shows an alternate route from the motorway he's on now. Which could save him time and miles. This outskirt town which would take off twenty miles from the motorway route. From what he judges on his map. Could be useful? The town is called Plockwell. It's late afternoon now. He may as well take the detour. ... There's a vague unease inside him that maybe it would be better to just stick to the motorway. But he's used up a lot of fuel thus far, far more than he'd anticipated, and if he can knock off some clicks then it'd be helpful in the long run. So then he's approaching a sign for PLOCKWELL on the left and he turns in and enters this new voyage. ... Emerges into this new place he's never encountered before. Scanty warehouses with concrete fields and sad fencing. A coal factory, brown and barren, abandoned. ... Then houses start to appear and they are classic council-housing, three storeyed, row on row of the same building. There's a long street of nothing but those and then a crossroads and the traffic lights there are not turned on – all the circles are grey. Anthony continues in a straight direction. Then he passes a bar. He knows it's a bar because there's a beer logo sign hanging above its main entrance. But, ehh, the building is burnt. Utterly blackened: the walls and the interior are all sooty and it looks like some battle partook in its car park. The locals burned the bar down? ... Anthony's window is opened a sedge and he gets a whiff of charcoal and carcinogenic plastic and he winds the screen up to the top. *I was an idiot to come into this place. Should I stop and go back to the motorway?* Just as he's thinking this, there appear a gabble of people from a street ahead of him. Anthony flickers. It's just a group of children. Tots. Must be under ten – not much of them either – but he'd rather not stop here in front of them and do the reverse and so he keeps going down the stretch. ... And he gets to this courtyard/square like area where he meets far more people, far older than those kids. Adults. Twenties, probably. At a glance he can't suss how many of them there are but it's far more than twenty; lounging around the benches and walls of the courtyard. ... When they see his van their heads clock on to him carnivorously. ... "Shit," Anthony whispers. Many people on the roads too. They're drinking and smoking. A bunch of them are sitting on the road right in his way ... and Anthony must slow his pace and corner around them and he

82

catches snaps of their faces as he passes them. Men and women. Mucked and drugged up, plied there in the middle of the road. … Anthony's slowing down was a display of cowardice. And the multitude has noted it. And the people from the courtyard start to skip closer to the van. … The road does not run north from here. There is only the one right turning at the end, a single route. And so Anthony cannot plough on. The folks from the sidewalks begin to come down onto the road too. And block its passage when they do. … Their frames are lost in the oblivion of substance abuse. Straggled hair and domino bars of teeth and wrecked clothing.

They continue to press against the van. Anthony has never been sure whether he's a coward or not. Sometimes, perhaps. Ultimately, no. This van is basically his house, now. Has everything dear he owns inside it. Now around thirty intoxicated mammals are threatening it. They keep coming and they're getting the collective idea to stop his way through. He gets to the right turn and he makes it onto that but then the folks in front of him have formed a barrage. Terrific fun for them. There's a woman who knocks on his side window and it startles him and they all laugh. (Anthony is not a coward; he's just never seen himself as the antithesis of what that is, whether there's a term for it. What he does know, all too badly well, is the sound of rash mirth. Ever since he was a boy. It's among the worst of sounds: but he's so experienced with it that he's learned how to deal with it.) … Anthony accelerates. To show them he means to push through. And it's met with whoooooos from the crowd; they're liking that they're beginning to annoy him. Then Anthony's patience snaps. And he HONKS at them. Three times, to get the fuck out of the way. … There are moments of silence. And then something slaps into the side of his van. Then a bang bangs on his roof. … Then his side mirror rips off and a bottle smashes on the floor underneath. … Which excites them all into frenzy.

They throw whatever they have on them. One man tries to wrench the driver door open. It's locked. So he punches the window and the blow hurts his knuckles rather than the window and then he slaps the glass instead and Anthony's response to everything is to ram down on the horn and keep it there, and the loud noise actually works because a lot of them spark away from the vehicle. Which gives him space. And uses it and spunks forward and with the momentum of this, many of the others jump out of the way of him. All the whiles he's swearing and his cheeks are ruby and his eyeballs wet. "You total bunch of bastards! What have I ever done to you? Why are you attacking me!" ... Most of them flee his passage. But there's a line of them up front – a last guard – who stay there on the road, confident burly deranged and daring him to hit them with the van. And Anthony's thinking *these people have lost all of their morals or sense of pride or respect for man, if indeed they ever had any. 'Loss' isn't the correct word at all; they aren't even men or woman and know nothing about 'mankind' or humankind in this state. They're hungry bullies. And I'm not going to be dragged out of my house and mauled apart by a bunch of bullying scum. Not at this age. I'm not dying just yet.* ... Anthony accelerates. Stomps his foot down. And romps towards them and they stay there and the van edges and edges ... and those on the corners of the line dart away to the sides. A trio are left in the middle. They've stopped smiling, but are still militant. Have you ever thought about killing somebody? Is it such a ludicrous fantasy? That abnormal? Anthony's mind goes, quite intricately, factually, *if I keep going at this velocity and they stay in the way then I will kill them* and yet there's a wrath and self denial, or self destruction, rather. ... And two of the trio fly out of his track. The middle one and the middle-left. And the middle-right stays. It's another woman. She watches it zoom up. And she tries to dodge it at the final second. And she fails. Because there is this thud in the corner of his bonnet and then her body vanishes. ... Anthony looks to his side mirror, to see where she is behind, imagining her body on the floor. The mirror isn't there. He remembers that the side mirror is smashed and it's just hanging there from its wires now. So he can't know what's happened. ... That *thud* was a horrible one.

Despite all this, he has clear road now and he should keep pelting for his own survival.

And not take any moronic risks again. Should not have trusted in coming into a strange town. Taken a speculative detour. His van is even more trashed now.

For now, focus on getting out of this Plockwell nightmare. There is no further carnage or movement of any sort throughout the entirety of the town and his exit is fairly simple. Only those drawn out depressed streets with the monotone storeyed houses; bred dereliction, a ten-thousand-population-town left to be forgotten about. And these are the results of the dismissal. ...

Anthony reaches its border and leaves it. Takes a while for his chest to stop thumping. For the sweat to dry on his palms. ... But he re-finds the correct motorway eventually. As mad as the detour was, it's worked out, in a way, in the end.

RUBY-ROSE

She cycles all day. Through this random generator of weather forms. A confused climate, switching from sun to showers, cold to hot; barely knows where it's at. Ruby-Rose (as you know) isn't that old but even when she was a kid fifteen years back it was never as erratic as this. It even hailstones at one point. This gush of hailstones come in a mad cameo; Ruby-Rose dives into a bus stop she finds and the stones crash above her and it's all enjoyable, these white tyke pellets skittering everywhere she can see, the myriad clangour all around. Lasts for some time too and she sits inside waiting for it to stop and then she must wait for it all to melt down because it wouldn't be safe to cycle down. ... *Then* this wave of summery sun comes up, and does that for her. Despite it being October. Insanity.

By early evening it's still light and in a mellow cloudy mood and she's in this middleclass kinda area filled with flats with amber walls. So she's back in the city; and this part seems relaxed and it's also deserted and she ponders *I could find somewhere around here to stay for a while.* Ruby-Rose passes this kids' playpark. All multicolour ladders and monkeybars and what not, amid the boulevard of the street she's on. Decides to take a break here. ... She leaves her bike by the gate and then sits on the edge of the silver slide. And fishes in her bag and gets some oatcakes and eats some of those. The slide is so small: it's amazing how huge and wondrous they seem when one is little – how easy it is to deduce marvel out of sliding down a sheet of steel. ... She could never do the monkeybars in childhood. Arms weren't strong enough. The boys used to show off to her and try and get her to do it too (back in old country that is) and she didn't know why she got so much attention from them. Nor was she impressed by their climbing skills. The swings were her fave. She'd twist the chains on the swings around and around above her and then release it and whirl back around and then stand up all dizzy and giddy. ... There are swings in this park too. She wouldn't be able to fit in their baskets now.

Other memories trundle and weave as she bites into a new oatcake ... until there's a whooshing sound farther down the street. Which prevents her from chewing. She stands up and heads towards the fence, to see closer, and looks down. Movement. It's a car, moseying down the boulevard, right towards her. And, umm, the car is styled in fluorescent blues and yellows. She can't quite believe it, but, yes, it's a police car. And she can't exactly hide because the park is tiny and she cannot get back on her bike again and bail because they'll see her fleeing. ... All she does is return to the slide and sit back on it. Then spits the lump of oatcake out into a tissue and throw it away. Then puts the rest of the cakes back in her bag and zips her bag up and she starts shivering and she hopes that the police won't see her and drive on ... and then the police car arrives by the park and there are two people in it. It stops. Halts. Ruby-Rose looks ahead at it. It's quite close. The car and her are close, rather, and she sees the window being drawn down, and another's woman's face appears. And calls out to her:

"Hello there. You okay?"

It's weird to hear a human voice.

"Yes I am," Ruby-Rose calls out, "Thank you."

"Could you come a bit closer to us?"

"I was just eating some oatcakes. Taking a break from my cycle ride. That's all."

"Come closer to the car, please."

Ruby-Rose gets up and heads nearer and she goes through the gate and it's like being on camera and she's always hated that – being on film.

Both of the police are female. Policewomen. One has black-polish hair; the other's blonde: and the blonde one's the one who addressed her before and she speaks again now:

"What are you doing in these parts?"

"I'm only cycling through."

"So you're not from here?"

"No. Just paused to take a rest, is all."

"Where do you stay then?"

Ruby-Rose tells them her address. The policewomen tilt their eyebrows and they share a glance.

"That doesn't make sense," blond policewoman says.

"Well ... that's my address."

"That's the other side of the city."

"I know."

"So you're escaping the rioting there?"

"*Has* there been more violence there?"

"That's the reason then?"

"Yes. ... But, did my area flare up as well? There was some looting. Outside my flat ... and I panicked and I left."

"Right. Well – where are you on your way to?"

"I ... I honestly don't know. I'm improvising."

"I see."

"So is that all right? I was just gonna get heading on my bike – to go," and she heads back to the park –

"No, hold on a moment."

"Yeah? Okay?"

"When did you leave your place?"

"Early yesterday morning."

"So where did you stay last night?"

"I just camped out."

"Where about was that?"

"Ehh ... It was in a park. I can't remember the exact name of it. Just in a park by a pond."

Both women look at her with that cold fury only females can reproduce. In intensity. A natural dislike behind the pupils, a joy of power. Blonde woman is only berating her with questions for her own pleasure. And dark hair is only watching it for fun too. They have no objective reason for confronting her. (They're threatened by the exquisite beauty of this young woman they have before them: all of it quite subconsciously trained. They don't have the same lips or noses or eyelashes or elbow-build or bust or hips and the image of it is quite a slight to their imperfection. ... And moreover the trembly visage of the lady makes it better, for them. A fearful civilian. ... The policewomen know what's happening across the city. It's completely beyond their control. This pair are too afraid to patrol closer into the town and that's why they're out in this random bit where they didn't expect to find anybody and now they see this incongruous character.)

"You're not making a lot of sense, girl," blonde cop says.

"In what way?"

"Well ... you've come all this distance, and you have no plan. You left your flat. Just because there was looting?"

"Yes."

"But did they try and attack your flat?"

"Not specifically no."

"Hmm ... Well I don't think your travelling story is logical either. You must be a pretty good cyclist to have come this far in one day ..."

"Two days. ... And yes, that's probably the reason I've gone so far. I'm neat with a bike."

"Ha."

"What is it that you want from me, ladies? I'm doing nothing wrong."

They snuff their noses.

"Did you see anybody else so far?" blonde cop asks.

"I'm not sure what you mean?"

"Since you left your flat yesterday morning, have you seen anybody on your journey?"

"No, I haven't."

"Not one person?"

(And throughout the words she remembers the guff of that man's breath. The feel of the air on her thighs when he wrenched her jeans down ... the solid feel of the knife's handle when she first clasped it and knew she had to retaliate.)

"No. I just wanted to get away from my place, that's all. Please."

"You didn't see anybody on your cycle trip up here, out of all of these miles?"

"Nah!"

"Don't get angry."

"I Did not meet a single soul."

"*Right*. We get it. Thanks for your time. You didn't need to be rude."

" ..."

"Well. We wish you well on your journey, girlie."

The black haired one, who has remained silent the entire scenario, starts the car up again and then it moves on and the side window rolls up also. They exit. With Ruby-Rose standing there. And they saunter down the boulevard until they finish it. And go. ... Ruby-Rose and the playpark afterwards once more, just as silently colourful as before. She sits by her bag. And understands that those policewomen were toying with her. They could have driven past and left her be and yet they chose to be mean ... all to reap trivial mocking memories. *Hard to take such casual aggression* Ruby-Rose's mind goes *especially at this stage. But I have to embrace it.* ... The animosity is left now. She gets up off the silver slide and she goes to her bike and checks it and it's all cool. She looks back at the slide and wishes she still had the quizzical infantile urge to flume down it. Then leaves the park. Saddles up and pedals on.

MARVIN

Elisa starts coughing around noon. Marvin hopes that they're just random coughs. But they're not; they persist and worsen and grow continuous throughout the day.

"Let's stop for a while, Elisa," he says. Nearby them there's a small wall before a garden (they're in a clean suburb now with single homes. Not so big but detached.). "Come and sit on the wall." She sits by him and it looks as if she's just woken up, she's so lethargic. Marvin has some Aspirin in his bag. He only has the one sachet left and there are only seven pills in it. He takes one pill out and gives it to Elisa.

"What's this?" she says.

"Aspirin … here, drink it down with some water."

He hands her the bottle and she does so. … All around them there are wavy wafts of wet wind; spittle rather than proper rain. This suburban neighbourhood is very small, and so far Marvin has seen no signs of human occupancy. It's off-beat from the main city districts. They passed one newsagent on the way here, which was closed. And a tiny pub, also locked up. Seems like a place where folks in their sixties go to retire. Marvin's fairly sure nobody's here anymore. He needs to help Elisa.

"You're sick, Elisa … How ill are you feeling?"

"I'm pretty bad."

"A runny throat?"

"Yes."

"Do you mind if I touch your forehead?"

"Yes … I mean, no, I don't mind."

He feels her forehead. He's tentative about touching her, still. *She's not my child and it's not really my place to touch her.* The forehead is clammy and hot. She's obviously developing a fever. Or has one already.

"We can't go on if you're ill. We'll have to stop and let you get better. That's what we'll do."

"Where? Can we stop."

Marvin stands up from the garden wall. A wispy watery wind goes in his face. The wall Elisa sits on has an unimaginative garden; one rowan tree, whose berries are stale and flat and the leaves yellowing and stranded. Nothing until a green front door. It's a semi-large house … And beside it there's a gate which must lead into the back garden: he can see a line of fir trees over its head.

"Hang on a second, Elisa," Marvin says. He hops over the wall and he goes up the main path to the front door and he rings the doorbell. And waits. Elisa watches him. Then Marvin knocks on the door and calls, "Hello? Is anybody in?" And nothing happens. *Nobody is in this house. This sick girl needs some proper shelter for a while.* He turns around to Elisa and calls, "Come on, kiddo. Come with me." ... She wonders what he's up to. Elisa's too delirious to think about much and she's always liked this windy-spatter weather and she can barely decide on anything aside from to follow Marvin, this unusual man. Marvin goes towards the side-gate. He kneels down and analyses the intricacies of the locks. Can't get at them from this side. So Marvin approaches the fence beside the gate and he jumps up and grabs hold of the top and then uses his boot-grip to propel himself upward and then he's on the top of it and the fence is a bit flimsy and he worries that it might collapse under him and so he jumps down the other side and lands amid a collection of flower pots. Falls over onto his waist. Ha. But, he's crossed the border. Gets up. The side-gate has two bolts and neither of them are padlocked and he slides them open and then Elisa is there looking at him. He smiles. She smiles as well. He beckons her and she comes through the gate and he bolts it after her.

Then they're officially in the back garden of this stranger's home. It's far bigger than the front garden. With flowerbeds and assorted trees and so on; the fir trees beside them offer the only vibrant colour, as most of the plants in the beds are dead. ... Marvin inspects the back side of the house. On the nearer left there are patio doors. Leading on to what looks like a living room. Then there's a stained glass window beyond that which is probably a downstairs bathroom. And at the far end there's another pair of patio doors before a kitchen. *Hmm. None of these windows seem the correct one to break into. What about upstairs?* There's another stained one at the top and two others which must be bedrooms. But there's one right in the centre. Must be the stairway window. ... Marvin looks around the garden. There's a shed in the far corner and he goes over to it looking for news and the shed's door is padlocked. ... By the side of it though are leaned planks of timber and sand&cement bags. All this gear fixed up for some kinda building project, which the Crash interrupted.

Most importantly, there is a ladder.

Marvin lifts it out and he carries it across the garden to the centre part of the house and it's not that heavy or tall a ladder but it reaches far up enough to that central stairwell window. He stands on it at the bottom to make sure it has a firm hold.

(Elisa all the while is ogling, entertained.)

Marvin climbs the ladder and he gets to the top. Doesn't take him that long.

Then he reaches into his inside coat pocket and he knows that Elisa's eyes are on him. And he takes out his handgun. Elisa flinches when she sees it. He looks down to her.

"Holds your ears, Elisa. Hold your hands to your ears."

She does so. And she closes her eyes. Marvin pulls the trigger and the window bursts open. There is the initial hole and then a skittering of cracks like an elaborate maze and then the whole sheet collapses and it falls away down into the weeds of the garden below. … Most of it falls and leaves a sizeable hole in the lower frame of the window. Marvin zips the pistol back up in his coat pocket. He climbs up onto the ledge and he crawls through the hole and then he's inside this new house. … Glass speckles have rinsed across the stairs under him.

Marvin leans out of the window and addresses Elisa. She's standing now.

"Come up the ladder, Elisa."

"Okay."

Elisa climbs the ladder and she gets to the broken window patch and Marvin offers to help her but she declines and climbs in by herself.

For both of them the new air smells like musky cotton. A scent which would be homely if Marvin and Elisa were familial members: if they hadn't just broken in. Weren't intruders.

"What now, Marvin?"

"Let's go downstairs first."

Their soles scratch the glass on the stairs.

Marvin tries the lightswitch that he arrives by at the bottom step. It does not turn on. There's still light from the downstairs window and they go into the kitchen … and Marvin tests the tap by the sink, and it's working and flowing. And he cups his hands in the flow and drinks and then he fills up the bottle from his bag and he gives it to Elisa. "We've got lots of water, now, Elisa, you'll be fine." She drinks from it too. "We'll let you get some sleep and drink lots of water, and your fever will go away. Right?" She nods. "You wanna come through to the living room? See if there's a place you can lie down on?" Again she nods and she follows him down the corridor into this new room. There's a couch nearby her and she falls on it instinctively. She's comatose. Marvin takes his jacket off and he puts it over her. ... This girl might be quite severely ill. She lies there and she falls into a stupor almost instantly after he's put the coat on ... and her shoes are handing out of the end of the couch. ... And he takes her shoes off, this time without asking. And they are soaking. All wet. As are her socks. Which he slips off too. "Elisa, why didn't you tell me your boots were sodden?" She only murmurs. As a response. She's asleep and he shouldn't wake her. ... Marvin's coat isn't big enough for her whole body. Not quite. Her (now bare) feet are hanging out from the bottom. ... There's another couch across the other side of the living room and it has a salmon coloured sheet across it and he lifts that off and as he stretches it out it is way bigger than his coat and he puts it all across her body, feet and head and all.

And there's this dainty cheekbone upturned to him by the foreign pillow her head rests upon. He wants to kiss her cheek.

But he can't. That would be perverse.

She's resting. She has some Aspirin in her. She's dry. That's a start.

What else is in this house? There might be other items to help her. Marvin goes into the kitchen first. It's a pleasant one: nicely designed ... he checks the cupboards. ... He finds nothing in the way of food. But there are plates and pots and cutlery and some glasses left. So he picks up a pint glass and fills it with water and then slips back into the living room and lays it on the coffeetable by Elisa's couch. ... The windows are still alight with the last of the afternoon daylight, and so Marvin pulls the curtains shut, as to save her eyes. ... Then searches the kitchen again. The fridge is off but he looks in anyway and there is nothing inside save a tub of butter – which when he opens it has blue mould growing on it – and a half empty bottle of cheap white wine, which when he lifts off the top stinks of full vinegar and it makes him sneeze. And umm there's a packet of beetroot in the vegetable bit. He looks at the sell by date and it's a month out of date but the purple bulbs look fine. Marvin was never a fan of beetroot; he leaves all that stuff in the fridge. And moves on to the further cupboards. He finds a box full of papers; bank letters and family postcards, Christmas cards. Feels creepy going near these items and so he leaves them alone. There's a clunky blender under that ... alongside a tub filled with elastic bands and some pennies and batteries and actually a small box of matches too. Marvin pockets the last two items. There's nothing else to be found in the kitchen. So he goes into the hallway past the living room and he searches in the downstairs toilet. Finds one bar of soap …

Then goes upstairs. Amidst the smashed glass; he pulls the curtain over the hollow windowframe and continues onto the upper deck. There are bedrooms. Again, he feels like a criminal if he were to go into the bedrooms, so he avoids these, but perhaps there will be something in the upper bathroom? Inside he goes and there are white tiles, a posh bathtub. There's a cabinet above the sink and a new tray within that and he brings it down and searches in it and there are some razors and a rusty pair of nose-hair scissors … and some leftover sachets of pills. And he looks through these, hopefully. None of them are painkillers, and have obscure medical/technical names he's unfamiliar with. But right at the bottom there's a little plastic bottle, orange and white, and he turns it around and the label says Vitamin C. *Score.* He opens it up and inside there's a decent bunch of tablets. Vitamin C supplements. Ace. Marvin has no fruit in his bag/food supply, very little foods which can aid the immune system.

He takes the bottle back downstairs and goes into the living room quietly. Elisa breathes in a fairy downy rhythm. The Vitamin box says you're supposed to take two per day. But Elisa needs some vitamins fast and so he slips out three tablets, and he shakes her shoulder lightly. She opens her eyes.

"Hello Marvin," she says.

"Sorry to disturb you, Elisa. But you should take these," and he hands her the pills, "They're Vitamin C. They will help you out."

She accepts it and puts them in her mouth and then drinks and he hears the liquid go down into her stomach.

"Thank you."

"No worries," he says, "I'll let you sleep now."

She nods and lies down again. Marvin leaves the living room and he goes into the kitchen. And therein he fills up a glass of water because he can't think of any other action to do. He sits at the dinner table. Which is perverse. And he imagines what kind of family used to live here. Or were they just a retired couple?

He imagines the table top filled with steaming food and napkins … and these people sitting around him making trilling conversational cues and smiling. *This is a dodgy thought.*

Because I've never really experienced that. Been good with folks. Was never 'socialised' that way, with dinner tables and hot meals. So why am I imagining that now? I've never been part of any society, family, group. Now I'm in some classic familial place, which I've invaded, and I've got this young girl with me. And I'm fretting about her already. It's my duty to keep her safe. Will I be able to do that? Am I a real man? He sits at the table and the evening descends outside and the land darkens and he watches the sky and the saturation in the room depresses to this low purple colour wherein Marvin could be anybody in the world. He's tried. He should ease down a bit and try to sleep as well.

So he goes into the living room and he checks on Elisa. Her ribcage is still moving. Marvin lies down on the couch opposite her. (The one he took the salmon sheet off of earlier.) For now, it seems like they're safe enough. He can try to sleep. Let his mind shut down for a small episode. Allow that rite.

Marvin's body is too long for the couch's span. But it doesn't matter. He shouldn't complain. He lies and listens to the atmosphere of the room … and Elisa's breathing is already there. But there's this tiny clip-clopping noise which he becomes aware of too. Methodical, cling-clong, tingly. He looks up, following the noise. It's a little alarm clock that's set on the coffeetable. He just never noticed it before. Old fashioned lil alarm clock. Sweet. … The sound is extra vivid, in the darkling situation. But it's also comforting. It lullabies Marvin away.

ELISA

She blinks into the fabric; a puddle stain of saliva under her mouth. Her body's too numb to move. Her tonsils were sore before. They're *throbbing* now. Her skull aches as well. Yes, there's nothing good to report. She stays on the same side, breathing, for what seems an aeon. And she zigzags between sleep and snippets of dreams and it's all hopelessly hellish. Then there comes a chapter where she can move, a bit, because she needs some water. And she gets up and her body feels as if it weighs tonnes … and Marvin has left a glass out for her on the table and she sups at it. And the water's swell in her mouth but it hurts with each gulp and she can only manage a small amount.

Marvin is asleep on the other side of the room. He does not look (whilst sleeping) any different. Neither peaceful nor animate. He's just solidly there. *But there are no covers on him and I feel bad because he keeps giving me his coat as a cover.* And she already has this salmon coloured quilt thing over her as well as his jacket. … So Elisa gets up from her couch and she lifts his jacket off of her. And when she stands up her brain chemicals sway and she stays still until they steady and then she goes to the other couch and puts the jacket across Marvin's body. … He mutters and breathes. *I love Marvin even though I don't know him so much.* Her temples shake from the fever. There's this constant swirl of saliva in her gums.

She gets back to her own couch.

I love Marvin. That's enough. He loves me as well.

Elisa sleeps for four hours afterwards without waking, whilst the disease flumes and emboldens throughout her body.

Marvin awakes early morning, when it's still dark, and he sits there watching her. *She put my coat back over me.* She is still sleeping and she needs it more and he drops it back over her and then he goes into the kitchen again. And he looks onto the garden. And it allures him and he opens the window that onlooks it. Marvin climbs through the window and goes out onto the grass and the wind is peppery and strong but he likes the way it makes flickering shapes on the grassblades … and as he goes forward he walks into a clothesline peg and it catches him by the neck. Idiot, slapstick – he didn't see it in the gloom. It nabs his windpipe and it's sore for a minute and then it's forgettable. He envisions a whole load of dresses and shirts on the clotheslines. In the future. That the family of this place will return. That it will all be restored. He hopes so. That they won't mind so much about the violent entry. … Marvin climbs back into the kitchen. Shuts the window down. And he turns around and there's a figure lurking in the doorway.

Elisa.

He jumps.

"Elisa … You okay?"

"Yes."

She's standing there. Fully clothed apart from her bare feet.

"I heard noises," she says, "and I didn't see you in the room, so I wondered where you were."

"Sorry to wake you … I went into the garden, is all. You should get back to the couch, Elisa."

"I'll try."

"Would you like some food?"

"No, thank you, though."

"You should eat something, Elisa. It will help."

"I know … I don't feel hungry at all though."

"Some more Vitamin C tablets, then?"

"Sure."

They go into the living room again and he hands her the tablets and she swallows them and drinks from the glass. And Marvin notices the glass is shallow and so he fills it up in the kitchen again and when he returns, Elisa is rummaging at her bag at the end of the couch. She's trying to find something inside. Then, as Marvin's coming nearer with the water, she brings out this object wrapped in a bandanna. And she undoes the bandanna and there's this notebook which appears.

"Marvin," she says, and she's holding a pen too. He's only just noticed.

"Yeah?"

"Would you write in my diary?"

"This is your diary?"

"It is," and she hands it to him. This delicate thing. He opens it up. Sifts through the pages and there is this wonderful array of spidery handwriting. Glossy and skilful and it looks purely artsy on the pages.

"But I shouldn't read your diary," Marvin says.

"I asked you to *write* in it."

"It's your diary, kiddo. I don't want to mar it with my idiot brain. I'm not a poet."

"I want you to write in it. You're not an idiot at all. Why do you even think that?"

She takes the diary from him again and then opens a new page and she presents it right in his face and she says,

"Even if it's just your name. I'd like it in there."

He takes it back from her and he wonders what to scribe on it and Marvin's never been talented with words (or anything in any domain or medium, for that matter) ... and so he writes his name in the open page of her diary, which seems to him this enormous space, and she watches him do it and it's as if he is the 8 year old and she the 29 year old, their roles reversed.

"I don't have much of a vocabulary, Elisa, is all," Marvin says, and he gives it back to her, "I'm no wordsmith."

"That doesn't matter, Marvin. Thanks."

"Okay ... But you need to get back to sleep now."

"I do."

She gets under the pink cover again and it doesn't seem to Marvin enough cover and so he goes upstairs into one of the bedrooms (breaking the taboo) and he finds a podgy quilt left there on one of the beds and he picks it up and he takes it back downstairs and goes into the living room and he drapes the quilt over her. (Elisa's awake when he does this. And she wishes that Marvin would get in beside her on the couch, to sleep. Just to sleep. So she would feel his bodyheat. And she's hoping, as he watches her from above, that he would do that. ... And she's sad that he crosses to the other couch after the poise ... That she was silly in thinking he wanted to sleep next to her too.)

ANTHONY BURTON

Anthony Burton goes through the bad things he's done in his life. Everything he can think of. From boyhood onwards, he lists the wickedness.

His mother Mandy used to give him a bit of pocket money each week when he was a kid. And usually he used it to buy soccer stickers, of soccer players that is, which he liked to collect in his folder at home. With the remaining coins he had left he bought sweets and pop and crisps and so on – so going to the newsagent was heavenly. He must've been about seven or eight. And went into the newsagent one weekday evening. And there was this new 'deluxe' or 'silver' set of soccer stickers that he really really wanted. The pack was just glorious and he had to have it. But it was twice the price. And he knew that his pocket money stipend wouldn't be able to cover the price of it. *But, it's only a few coins more* he thought. Anthony knew where his mother kept her purse. Or rather – she had a habit of leaving it by the phone in the kitchen and he just knew it was often there. … Mandy gave him the pocket money on a Friday afternoon when he got home from school. And she did so this Friday as normal. And he waited until she'd gotten drunk on wine in the evening and she was outside in the garden reading a book. And he took his chance and he robbed a few coins from her purse. And succeeded. At first, or so he thought. And sneaked upstairs and hid them under his bed and hoped that she wouldn't notice that they were gone. Then on the Saturday morning he went up to the shop with the pocket money and the thieved coins and he bought the deluxe soccer stickers and he felt as if he were being spied on the entire way and that he would be caught out any moment. He opened the packet on the way home and the stickers were incredible. And he thought he'd stick them in a special jotter, as to preserve them. … And he got home and went through the front door, thinking that his crime was complete. And Mandy was standing, *towering*, right there in the hallway, staring at him. He blushed, and closed the door, and he couldn't look at her. "I know what you did, Anthony," she said. "Come over here." He went over to her. Under her. She was huge. "Show me what you bought with my money," she said. He took out the deluxe stickers and she snatched them off of him. Then she bent down and said, "Hold out your hand." And he knew what was coming and held the hand out, and she slapped it.

Anthony never got slapped in the face or anywhere else – it was always the hand, and was sore enough to let him know that he'd mucked up. She told him to go up to his room and stay there until she told him he could go out again. And that's what happened. ... ... All day and unto the evening he thought he was the worst boy in the world. That he'd be disowned. That he'd never be forgiven, that he should run away from home. Then when it was twilight there was a soft knocking on the door. Mandy came in. He was afraid; she sat on the end of his bed. And told him not to steal from her purse ever again. And that she was not going to give him any pocket money next Friday. But on the Friday she would give him his deluxe stickers back. The agreement being that he would not rob anything again in his life. Was that a deal? Yes. She smiled, and said he could leave his room if he wanted to. And he said sorry and she accepted it. And next Friday when he got his stickers back he still felt guilty. ... That was fine parenting.

There's another one from when he was younger than that. Far worse.

Five years old. Anthony was playing by himself in the home garden. And he noticed this worm squirming about in the soil. He picked it up and inspected it. And he'd heard something in school at class (because they were doing a project on insects, as a topic, learning about insects) whereby worms, if they happen to lose a section of their body, if their tail is cut off, then they are naturally able to grow it back again. Can regenerate. And Anthony was curious about this idea. He wasn't sure whether it was playground myth or genuine fact and he was interested in discovering, and so he laid the worm out on the garden bench and he went into the kitchen and got a butter knife and came back out ... and he severed the bottom end of the worm off. Just hacked off a chuck of its body. And his stupid imagination expected it to grow in front of him and heal itself. It twitched and shuddered. ... Anthony *knew* that it was all playground bullshit. Nor was he thick enough to really think the worm would survive after he did that: he was only being sadistic. He just wanted to kill something. Without being reprimanded for it.

In Anthony's same school there was this 'mentally impaired' or 'mentally disabled' kid. So he might have been heavily autistic or something like that; he was unable to defend himself like neurotypical kids, didn't have any cruelty or knowhow with words or fists. ... There's no background to this story: Anthony just jumped him one time in the playground. For no reason. Without any provocation. He saw the boy as a target (Justin was his name) and attacked Justin, tackled him, pushed him down onto the floor, and Justin screamed and called out for somebody to help him but there was nobody around, no adults or kids either. Then Anthony got off of Justin and left him sobbing on the ground. … And Justin went and told one of the supervisors about it later on and Anthony was spoken to about it by one of the teachers. He was given a 'danger mark', and ordered to apologise to Justin. And that was it. That was the first and last time Anthony 'beat somebody up'.

Fastforward to high school. Anthony had this girlfriend, first girlfriend ever. She had wonderful hair and her breasts had grown rosy from a young age and they did the halcyon early chapters whereby they learned each other's bodies, smells, exploring erotica. … Then after six months they realised they didn't have much to talk about and she got fussed about it and moved away from him. So he broke it off with her. And broke her heart. And then she realised that she still liked him and wanted him back. And this happened around Halloween and Anthony sensed that she still had feelings for him, and he remembered all of that sexy stuff (despite them never having had proper sex) and he wanted those feelings back and so he invited her out on a date and he kissed her and suddenly they were back together again. He didn't want to stay flaccid for the winter, and he didn't have any proper feelings for the girl but he got back with her just for the selfish fun of it. So there were a few months of further kissing. And he got her to take her bra off and they would kiss in this alcove in the city, this dark place under a stairwell in a backstreet, and he would feel her hard nipples versus the harsh December air. But they were still only fifteen and didn't know how to have sex and they couldn't exactly do it here. … She would come over to his house on the weekends a lot and they would make out on his bed and watch films. (Which his parents totally despised.) And it was in the week leading up to Christmas. They were sexually charged in bed and the film was playing in the background, with excessive kissing and fondling, and she finally managed to reach into his jeans and boxers and rub his erect penis. Anthony came in under forty seconds. She didn't even unbuckle his belt and he just left his warm jism there in his boxers. … So after all this time he'd gotten what he wanted and it amounted to 40 seconds and he realised he didn't love this girl at all. He got up from the bed and focused on the TV, the film, because he found it more interesting than her. And within the first week in January he broke it off with her. She fucking hated him after that. Quite rightly so.

Anthony regurgitates all these memories as he drives.

Do these examples sound like the deeds of a moral person? I've thought I was a good man. A wise man, for some time. I'm in my early sixties now and for long I've believed I was a decent person.

Am I really?

There are four stories above and none of them sound like the protagonist is a hero.

These examples all came in youth. And there is that element of wisdom whereby 'people do stupid things when they're young and they can be forgiven for it'. But is this really the case?

He's approaching a new night now. It's been weird driving without a side-mirror. Anthony feels like he's losing concentration – and after all that's happened to his van in recent times, he's driving slower and anticipating something else. ...

Anthony's on the correct motorway. And it shouldn't take him that much longer to finally exit the metropolis boundaries. But he should sleep, lest he crash. And so he takes a quiet road aft the motorway, much the same as last night. He stops on the side of the road, aside a field. With no cattle or sheep or anything in it. And he takes out his pipe and smokes at it.

I am not a moral man. Never really have been, if I look at it. Don't even deserve this tobacco.

All this time, I have remembered the time when I beat up that autistic kid. And I've rated it as the worst thing I've ever done. ... Among many other bits/examples.

But I ran into a woman with my van earlier today. Hit her with my van. And she might be dead. Because of me. I didn't stop to see whether she was alive or not, and drove on like a coward. ... And so I'm still not a moral man. At 62. So why should I be granted a way out of this apocalypse?

Maybe I'll never escape. Will be murdered myself, yet. Why does an immoral man have the right to live through Armageddon?

RUBY-ROSE

Her best friend from back home Emma had a historical problem with feinting. Emma feinted a lot. It was her weakness.

Ruby-Rose first met Emma in nursery and that was when the first episode occurred. They were out in the playground behind the building (which was a disused church) and Ruby-Rose and Emma were among the small clique of girls that were amongst the nursery kids: all the rest were boys. And the boys would run around as much as they could, trying to attract the four girls that were near them, who hung out in the corner, unphased. (Why do males often think they have to show bravado in order to attract the girls – that they have to *perform* in public and do all this unnatural sport. Does that tactic ever work?) Anyway, the tactic to attract R-R and Emma and the other two that day was to play tig-tag in the yard. (Is that your term for the game? 'Tag'.) And they ran around tagging each other and they kept touching the girls on the shoulders and arms and wanted them to join in and the girls didn't get what the excitement was about and they didn't do anything. … This one boy had just been tagged … and it happened right in front of the girls, and embarrassed him, and he was keen on revenge, and so he raced after the boy that'd just tagged him and he was overly intent and he got him, but pushed rather than tagged. And the other boy fell over. Onto his knees. And he was wearing shorts. And his kneecaps skidded right into the concrete, and he instantly started crying. The tagger, knowing that he was a fiend, ran away. And left the boy to get up by himself. And the boy stood up. And when he fell he had bashed open his left kneecap. And this immense trail of blood steamed from it now. … Emma was standing next to Ruby-Rose. She saw the gore, and she just collapsed because she couldn't stand the sight of it. Ruby-Rose didn't even know what happened at the time. Emma crumpled and then she was on the floor … and then Ruby-Rose got upset and started crying because she pulled her friend up, wondering what was wrong, and Emma wouldn't wake up. She ran to the lady supervisors inside the nursery building, who were smoking cigarettes and drinking coffee and irritated to be bothered on their break from the kids.

Another time. When they were both older, Emma was invited out with Ruby-Rose's parents, to see a glossy sci-fi movie, on Ruby-Rose's birthday. They went down to the mall/complex and they had pizza before the movie, and her parents were fond of Emma, as everybody was. Then they went upstairs to the cinema. And got into the auditorium. And it was a cracking movie. It was all laser blasts and robots and goofy fun. … But there came thing one scene where this goblin/alien thing gets eaten/murdered by a larger alien thing … And the instant after that image of violence, Emma was suddenly on the floor. She'd dropped her popcorn box and the pops spilled all over the carpet with her and it was dark and the film was booming and so there was wide awkward confusion. R-R helped pick her up alongside her Dad, and she regained consciousness outside the theatre, after Dad splashed some cola on her face. Emma was humiliated that she'd spoiled the birthday occasion. Nobody said that was the case. But she still felt guilty. … R-R later asked her why she had feinted? And Emma coloured and said it was because she didn't like seeing that alien thing be eaten by the bigger alien. She was disturbed by it. Her mind couldn't handle it and she timed out.

Then the feinting stuff got a bit more serious. Later in life.

Because she blanked out in school (proper school, not nursery). Whence in P.E. class – the girls were getting ready for a swimming lesson and all of the girls had to change and get naked together in this small room and both R-R and Emma were scared about showing their bodies to the other girls. (So they would have been young teens at his point, when puberty was first arriving and they were nervous about the sizes of their breasts, their bodies in general.) … And R-R had noticed that Emma was moving drowsily and that she was struggling to keep her balance in the changing rooms. And the snooty snarkly sound of the other girls bitching about other bitches didn't help at all, the volume of that effeminate garble. … It was super hot in those rooms and R-R hated it as well. She asked Emma is she was cool. Emma said yes. They went out onto the pool side.

The P.E instructor was this young man who was only here to get some experience. He was camp. Was bubbly and likable.

The girls came out to meet him beside the swimming pool, on the sweating corners, the funk of chlorine. And inside the pool atrium it was even hotter than the changing rooms. … And Ruby-Rose saw Emma dunk her head, right beside her, as if she were about to fall asleep, in her pathetic bikini, with her small tits which she was ashamed of because all of the other girls had bigger ones. … And then Emma feinted.

And she cracked her head pretty bad on the tiles. And the cap P/E guy and Ruby-Rose freaked out at the exact same time. Because she landed with such a perfect, cinematic slap of the cranium.

Emma was concussed. There triggers for the latest feint had been the he and the nasty exterior social pressure. ... Emma was taken to hospital for a while and was discharged shortly afterwards.

Ruby-Rose went to her home the next day to check up on her. Emma's parents let her into the house. ... R-R went up to Emma's bedroom. She knocked on her door. Emma called to allow her entry. A bandage was wrapped around her head.

"How are you, my friend," R-R went towards her.

Emma was sleepy and it took her a moment to realise who was with her and then she saw Ruby-Rose fully and her cheeks widened into a smile.

"Ruby? What's up?"

"I wanted to see how you were."

"I'm here ... I'm good."

"I was worried about you."

"Don't be."

"Does it hurt? Your head?"

"Nah, not really. They gave me medicine. I'm just drowsy is all."

"Can I stay in the room?"

"What do you mean?"

"Can I stay here while you sleep? I'd just like to stay."

"Okay."

"Okay, thanks."

Ruby-Rose initially sat down on the chair in front of her bed. Emma tutted. And said, "Come and get in with me, Ruby," and she lifted her covers up. Ruby-Rose got in beside her. Soft. Warm. Physical. Exhilarating. She hugged her friend. Emma embraced her back.

PART THREE

MARVIN

Day two in the house that they've broken in to. Marvin shuts pulls the blinds on the kitchen window and he keeps the door leading onto the living room open a crack. For hours that day he sits in the dimness listening to Elisa cough in the next room. And he wishes he could be of more help. The Aspirin is running out. Handful of tablets left – and he know he should ration them for her. He hopes that since she's only a kid then they'll be powerful enough to ease the pain. They don't seem to be working. Her coughing is a staccato rapping sound, like a flat object being slapped against water. You can't sleep when you cough. It gets beyond noon and unto the mid afternoon and it shows no signs of abating. He does bring her fresh glasses of water. And spaces out the Aspirin doses. Her face sweats, and sucks air harshly through her mouth with her nose all bunged up. *… I have to do something about this child; try harder to make her better.* So Marvin explores the house again, looking for further items that may be of use. There's one room upstairs. A door. Which when he tries it is locked. Marvin imagines it must be a study or something like that. He goes into one of the bedrooms and there is a chest of drawers and he opens that and there are only clothes hangers and the room is totally scant … aside from when he looks under the bed and he finds a left-over toilet roll. *That's something at least – that's something for her to cough and sneeze in to.* Because he only has the one roll in his bag left. … He tries the next bedroom which was obviously the main couple's one because it's huge and has a king size bed … and it's also derelict aside from this old fashioned TV in the corner. But the noticeable thing it this unsettling smell. Perfume or disinfectant – a chemical nuance he cannot bare – and he really doesn't want to search this couple's room and so he leaves and shuts the door. There is a cupboard in the middle of hallway. Inside this he finds a hoover, and for some reason a stack of classic board games on the floor. But there are quilts and towels in there, and leftover pillows. All of which could be beneficial. He takes the latter bits downstairs and sneaks into the living room as quietly as he can and looks down at Elisa. She's sleeping. Or so it looks like, her back softly liftlurching. He leaves the towels and pillows by her couch. Then goes into the kitchen and sits at the table.

Marvin's hungry but shouldn't eat any of the food they have

left. He wonders *maybe I could take a walk outside in the neighbourhood, just to mosey around, climb through the window again. But I shouldn't leave Elisa in the house alone. Plus, I might meet some other maniacs if I dare to go out again. It's possible.* ... And so he sits. All he can do is think.

He thinks about the present. This constant hum of tension that has lagged on for so long. Believes that he's dealing better with the panic of all of it. Or is it perhaps that the break of sitting in this dark peaceful room (despite everything else that's happening) allows him to relax in this ironic way. ... Marvin also thinks about his past. Memories which he often used to get furious about. Before the Crash happened. As he's sitting in this new situation he finds that those memorial woes aren't so poignant anymore. He can't get angry about them as much. In this small scene, within this room. Because they're all insignificant considering the context he's in now.

The violence and animosity of his past have chipped and cracked away at him. But he's too fatigued for them to bother him now. Anger and fury can never be creative, in any long term way. ... Those fuels are mercurial. They can be entertaining. But are ultimately useless. Is that what makes the present different? That Marvin's being creative with his life, in trying to save this girl Elisa? Rather than wallow in Time and History. Expecting time and history to change or do something differently for you; expecting those forces to lessen their damage from their own end: these are impossible feats. Time and history dictate. People are nothing compared to their vast scales. Their scales are incompatible. ...

Why not just allow the mind a bit of rest, once in a while. In spite of all that's been done to you.

Marvin falls asleep in the kitchen on the chair by the table with his head against the wall.

He awakes with a gushing noise hours later. He stands up. Thinking something's wrong, and panics. Gets up from the table and rushes into the living room, and Elisa isn't there on the couch. Her covers are pulled down. Then she comes back into the room, very slowly. The noise that woke him up was the downstairs toilet flushing. She looks up at Marvin. A tiny smile. Then she heads back down to the couch and falls under the covers. He kneels by the couch. She closes her eyes. Her whispers to her if she would like anything to eat. He can make her some food. She says thanks but she still can't stomach anything.

"But, Marvin?" she says.

"Yes?"

"You don't have to stay in the kitchen."

"I don't want to bother you, is all."

"You don't have to sleep in the kitchen. You can be in here with me."

"I don't want to keep you up."

"You won't keep me up. You'll help me sleep."

"… How are you feeling Elisa?"

"Like hell. If you please just stay on the couch by me, I'll know that if I need help, then it's right there."

"Okay. I'll stay."

Marvin goes into the kitchen and he fills up the water glasses. Unto the living room and he lays down on the other couch. Elisa's quietened. Her head is to the back of him and. He lies. The pillows under his back are saintly. He sleeps.

She hears this mad tumbling sound with all kinds of polyphony notes. The sound is in her dream and then she awakes and her throat feels as if it can't reap any air and she coughs and coughs and tries some of the water and the mad sound is still there. In her delirium it's hard to suss what it is. Birds. Birdsong.

"Marvin?" she whispers out in the dark.

"Yes? What's up?"

His shape comes across to the coffeetable and he sits down aside it.

"Can you hear them, Marvin?"

"Hear what?"

"Birds!"

"No … I can't make them out. What do you mean?"

"The birds are singing."

Marvin watches her with a developing fear.

"Do you mean from the garden, Elisa?"

"Must be that, yes."

"But it's the night time, Elisa. The birds are all sleeping."

"I can honestly hear them. Their singing is amazing."

"…"

"Can you do me a favour?"

"Uh hu?"

"Can you open the kitchen window?"

"Why?"

"So I can experience that magic sound a bit more."

"You'll get cold."

"I won't. I'm already boiling under all these covers. Please. Just do me that favour."

"Elisa … you need to go back to sleep."

"Please."

"Okay. But will you promise me one thing in return?"

"What's that?"

"That you try and eat something? You haven't eaten in two days. Is that a deal? I open the window, you eat a bit of food."

"Right. Sure."

Marvin goes through to the kitchen and he heads to the window and opens the blinds. *Are there actually birds singing? Is Elisa right?* And he leans close to the window to check whether she's right. It is indeed perfect black night. Through the window the garden trees sway indifferently. He opens the

110

window from the bottom half and the wind whisks his face. Marvin peers outside and watches the outlines of the trees. Listens. There's the myriad lush rippling of leaves, dead and alive, and the presence of the murky air itself. But, birds? He knows the lyrical joy of birdsong well. And his mind would like to imagine those sounds now and he stays in this curious universe for some time, listening. But fears that if he stays too long then his mind will start to hallucinate as well.

But, he's done his bit. Time to get some food for Elisa. He gets one of the left-behind bowls from a cupboard and from his bag he still has some tinned food. One of the tins is pineapple. Sliced pineapple rings and he always liked those when he was little and even though it's tinned food there must be some nutrition left in them. Spills the juice out of the can in the sink. Gets a knife and fork. Cuts the slices into smaller pieces and then takes it through to Elisa. She's already sat up on the couch. She takes the plate with a twitchy hand.

"Thanks for the birds," she says.

"No problem. Try some of the food."

She puts a slice in her mouth.

Elisa doesn't want him watching her eat. And he gets that vibe too – he never liked being stared at when he was supposed to perform. So he goes into the kitchen again. *When will we be able to leave this house and get back on the road again* he wonders. *What will we do when we finally get out of the city? Perhaps I could be a guardian to Elisa. Be her guardian. If she wanted me to be. There are towns up north that have stable economics. I can support Elisa financially for sure. It's always possible. ... We'll get through her fever. It'll pass. We'll do a bit more travelling and then we'll be out and away. That's the way the future will go.*

She calls him. He comes to her. She's holding out the plate and it's empty.

"Good effort, Elisa. You feel better?"

"I do. Thanks."

He takes the plate into the kitchen and puts it by the sink and comes back to her.

"You want to try and go back to sleep?" Marvin says.

"I can't right now."

"Okay."

"But ... can I tell you something?"

"Of course. Go on."

"I keep thinking about my Mum. She keeps coming back to me … In my memory I mean."

"Where is your Mum, Elisa?"

This was the wrong question for Marvin to ask. Because Elisa's face winces up and her eyes prickle as if she's about to start crying. Marvin shouldn't have said that.

"Sorry, Elisa. Tell me whatever you want to say."

And luckily Elisa doesn't cry. She talks, instead. In this pixie voice, in fragments, cloudy sentences.

"We had to leave the house. Mum was panicking. More than me. We were trying to get down to the train station. To escape, and she had booked tickets … she couldn't stop speaking in this shrill voice like she was going crazy. It was night time. She took too many bags with her to carry to the station. And gave too many to me hold as well.

"So in the streets there was all this smashed stuff and I was scared of it and the bags were heavy for me. And she kept shouting at me to hurry up, hurry up, even though she was feeling the same way and strained herself. … And I said, 'Mum, I can't carry all this stuff by myself.' And she said just keep trying. But I had to stop because my arms and back were hurting. And complained again that I couldn't do it. And then she screamed at me and said we'll have to leave some of the bags behind '*Thanks very much, Elisa*!'. And her words hurt me too and I hated her a bit. And so we left the bags of the pots behind. And the bag of dry food. Potatoes and rice and spaghetti: Mum had put them all in one bag and it was by far the heaviest and it was causing the most effort. She still believed that we would catch the train and that it wouldn't matter if we left all this uncooked food. We could buy more when we were somewhere else. And we bailed on her bag of books too. Which was precious to her but not needed. We just abandoned them on the road."

Marvin hears her with exhilaration. The single spectator of a soliloquy. Elisa's only audience. It's just brilliant to hear. This outburst of therapy. His fingers tingle.

She's quiet for a period. She drinks from her glass.

Then she hesitates before continuing. Because she still can't see Marvin's face; cannot peg the way his face moves alongside her story. His shape is stark and physical. But she can't discern his emotions.

"I'm here, Elisa," he says, "keep going with it. I'm listening."

"We walked in silence for a long time. Mother was a pretty lady. She had this hair which swished a lot … and even when she was angry it was something to look at. Mum walked ahead of me and her hair flipped about her shoulders. And I thought that she was still raging. But then she stopped in one of the streets. And she took out a bottle of water. And I stopped behind her and I was worried about going close to her. She looked down at me. And her face changed.

"She bent to me and kissed me on the cheek and she said, 'I'm sorry about yelling at you earlier. I'm just terrified, is all. But I shouldn't have taken it out on you.' And I remember hugging her when she hugged me and I felt her ribs on her back and they were so thin. And I thought, *when I grow up will I be as brittle as she is*? 'Let's just catch this train, Elisa, okay?' she said. – 'Okay, Mum. But we've got enough time to get there. We don't need to rush so much.' I said. And she said that we needed to hurry rather than rush. And she raced out in front of me and I had to race after her again.

"We went into the big town bits. And the damage there wasn't as bad. Everywhere was shut but the streets were cleaner. And I thought we were going to make it.

"Mum got to the top of the tall long staircase which led down to the train station. A steep scary case of stone steps. Dangerous. I said to Mum 'Be careful on the steps'. But she did not listen. She carried on. And jumped down the steps fast as she could. She was still crazy. I called her back. Told her to stop. And I was trying to keep balance on the stairs myself. And I got mad myself, and screamed after her. And it was like she wasn't even listening. She ran on and on down the steps farther away from me.

"And she tripped. And fell. She dropped her bags … and they flew away from her down the steps. Mum fell down the steps like a plastic toy. Bash bash bash on the little figure body. She had no control over her balance. And she landed with a smack, on one of those straight bits. After the stairs. What do you call them? You know what I mean, Marvin?"

"The landing bits between the stairs."

"Yes. And she hit her head on the landing bit. And stayed still. I got down to her. She landed on her front. As in, it was her face that she landed on. And I still remember that hollow sound it made, when it hit. … So I pulled her up and over onto her back. And there was this gash somewhere under her hair. With blood running from it. Her eyes were shut. I screamed a lot and my echoes spun up and down the stairs. … I brought a tissue out and tried to plant it on the place on her head where it was bleeding. I couldn't really find it. And the tissue was useless. Then I reached under her neck, to the side of her throat, to feel if her pulse was still there. And I kept pressing and pressing. But there was nothing. Her neck wasn't even warm at all. Even after this rushed journey. I asked her to get up. I said, 'Please try and get up, mother. Please get back up.' But she couldn't. She didn't. I held her cheeks and tried to lift her eyes open with my fingers but she wouldn't move again."

"I'm so sorry, Elisa."

"But the worst part was what happened right afterwards. Because I was kneeling next to her. And I heard this noise come from the top of the stairs and I looked up and there was a band of people. Coming down the stairs. They were far off. And I got terrified. I thought that if they saw me with this bleeding woman then they might think that I pushed her down the stairs. That sounds silly now but that's what I thought at the time. I thought that they might call the police on me. And that I would be trapped here. And then taken away and that I wouldn't be believed if I told anybody what happened.

"And so *I* panicked. And I touched her hair one last time. I brushed it out of the smear of sweat on her face and tucked it behind her ears. Don't know why, that's just what I did.

"I knew that the train tickets were in her jean pocket in her purse. So I lifted her purse out of that and I found my ticket. There was some cash in the purse and her bank cards and so on. I didn't want the people who were coming down the stairs to rob her. So I pocketed her purse. … I didn't even say anything to her before I left. And like an idiot I didn't think to pick up any of the other bags that she had dropped, and that I had put down. There was one with sandwiches and fruit in it that we'd made for the train journey and I was too stupid to pick it up as I ran away. All the while the band were coming closer and I didn't want to know who they were and I never even saw them fully and I got to the bottom of the stairs and ran across the street and through the train station gates. There was this group of pigeons right there before the gates and they got a fright when I arrived and they sprang up and I had to duck one of them else it would've whacked into me.

"The train station was weirdly quiet. I ran down the overhead tunnel and I got to the public bit and the first thing I noticed was that one of those soda dispenser things – what do you call them? – the drinks machine or whatever. It'd been knocked over and all of the cans of pop had gone everywhere and there were these mass brown pools of cola and milkshake … which I ran over. And I went down this next set of stairs into the main atrium and I'd expected to see hundreds of folks about. Waiting in the main square for their trains. But from the top of the stairs I saw almost nobody there. Only a few folks running about. And I wondered what was up. The stairwell had a few flights and I ran down and down and I got to the last flight and at the bottom of that there were four policemen standing there. I shrieked.

"Because I wasn't expecting them. I thought that they were waiting there for me, to arrest me. For what happened with my mother. This sounds retarded too but that was what I thought. These four men. All of them were fat. Out of shape. But when I saw them and I shrieked, they all flinched. And looked up at me. Curious. Then there was this standstill where I thought they would come up the stairs and put handcuffs on me. And it was one on four. A cop stepped forward and spoke to me, saying, 'What are you down here for, girl?' I said I had to catch a train. He said there were no trains. The station was shut. 'But, I have a ticket. For this train. It's in twenty minutes.' He told me that the station was closed and that there were no trains.

"I pulled out the ticket and I went down the stairs, not believing or understanding what he was saying … I didn't get why the whole station would be shut. And I thought that my ticket would let me through. … He swore at me. Told me to fuck off. And he pushed me over. I think he meant to push me back but I wasn't expecting his touch and then I was on the floor. … The other cops just watched. They went silent for a moment after I fell. Then when they saw that I wasn't hurt badly, they didn't react in any way, and the cop that had pushed me walked back to them. And I went back up the stairs. And out of the station."

Elisa stops the fable and she leans against the back of the couch.

Marvin's astonished by her tiny voice. Marvin did not know his own parents well. Could never have developed a love for his father or mother because he spent so little time with them. Now there's this little girl telling this horrific story, it kind of cushions his brain. Makes him think differently; extends a philosophy.

Makes him wish he wasn't such a bad person in the past. That both of the people are so small in the world and yet that this girl is far better than he is. She has a finer soul, spirit. Moral. Innocence.

Elisa, having said all this, yawns down into her covers.

"That's a brutal story, Elisa," Marvin says.

And it's *then* that she starts crying. She doesn't make noise. But she turns around the other way on the couch and buries her face in the corner … and her whole frame shakes, flutters, the frail shoulders twinkling under the linen.

Marvin wonders how to react. He remembers that he's no poet, not good with words, not really good at anything, if he looks at it objectively. He's 29 and he's never achieved anything astounding. What's he doing with his life? He should have some powerful line to try and console Elisa. But he's too thick to do that. Reserved, boyish. And so what he decides to do is put a hand on one of her shoulders to stop it shivering. It's like touching a ball-like old-fashioned door handle. Brass muscle and bone. And she relaxes by his touch. … Marvin can't remember the last time he wept. It's just not something that he does. Probably a touch of that macho garble. Or rather that securitised arena of masculinity which is excellent at harbouring rage and stubbornness and the root of vengeance. It's easier to build a dam off of those themes. Even when nobody's looking. Or when he was in his bed at night, in the past, whence younger and thinking about all the things that bothered him, all the scars he had … it was easier to keep that dam up. No matter how huge the abyss was. … Marvin really really wants to cry right now as he holds Elisa. He wishes he were a proper man, without a boyish past. Wishes that he could have saved Elisa already.

Elisa stops weeping.

Then she turns her head around to him.

It is not shiny or relieved, rather retired and damaged.

"Please tell me how I can help you, Elisa?"

"You've already helped me enough, Marvin. You are a good man."

"We're friends, right?"

"Of course."

"So you won't leave me will you? I'll help you get through this and you won't depart? You won't go away from me?"

"Never ever …"

Marvin takes up her glass, which is running low on water,

and he fills it up in the kitchen tap. And brings it back to her. And she says thanks. She holds his hand as she says this. Then turns around again and curls back up into the corner.

ANTHONY BURTON

The clouds through Anthony's Burton's bashed windscreen are bruising with all kinds of colours. He's stopped his van. Smoking the pipe. He can smell his sweat through his shirt. Rancid body odour, ripe as if he were a teenager. Needs a shower. And no wonder: the thermometer on his dashboard screen says 18°C. It's that warm, in the middle of an October afternoon, in *this* country! Senseless stuff. ... But the clouds bulge and ooze as if they're looking for vengeance. Maybe they are. They're stunning paintings, nice to watch; also dormant and they promise a showdown storm. It's kinda exciting, Anthony must admit, wondering just when they will break. He's also close to exiting the city. He's stationed right now before a turnpike which, if he goes down it, should take him (finally) out of the city boundaries and he can be free of this muck. Anthony can see the booths at the entrance of the turnpike. Which are empty of personnel. And the barriers – the pole gates where the traffic is supposed to stop – have all been bashed open and the poles are lying on the floor. All four of them on the quartet of traffic channels. Must've been rammed through some time ago when the turnpike keepers had vanished and folks were bailing. So he needn't worry about paying, or getting through okay. ... Anthony looks at his reflection in the one side mirror he still has. He could do with a shave as well. He doesn't want to be turning up to his friend's house in this state. Should try and clean up before he arrives. But, he's nearly there. *Just got to get out of this doomed metropolis first. Should not take long now.* He finishes the pipe. Then starts his van up and he drives up towards the turnpike turnstiles, and goes through the empty gate and his front and back wheels bump over the poles under him. Anthony sails onwards.

She notices the clouds, the humidity; knows there'll be a storm. It actually gives her incentive because her cycling has been robust yesterday and today and she's almost made it to the border of the city. Ruby-Rose thought it was just her passionate cycling that's been making her face drip all day. But it's obscurely hot, like it's midsummer. Almost as if there could be lightning tonight as well. … She's taking a break at the moment at the side of the road. She eats the last of her rolls. It's a bit stale and flabby but it gives her some calories and she's confident about a penultimate chapter in her journey, to cycle on and be unsaddled of the city. (As she eats her roll there are three seagulls high above her, prickly and hungry. These birds are total fiends. Nobody likes them. But she kind of feels bad for them. And she eats too fast and her gullet is satisfied and there's a little portion of the stale roll leftover. And so she chucks it out onto the road, for the gulls. They rip down to it, divebombing, with scary gusto. *If reincarnation exists* Ruby-Rose thinks *I hope I never turn out as a seagull in the next life.*) She gets up on her bike and pedals.

Industrial district. Industrial *atmosphere*: she bikes on a bypass and there are these stark depressed fields with their gutters/ditches all clogged up with driver litter. As if people enjoy vandalising them. Adding to the ugliness, just to make it worse. Factories. Cuboid buildings with funnels and slogans and security gates. Amongst these fields. … It's as if these parts have no clue of the Crash whatsoever, have been blindfolded the entire time, before and since. Only difference is that there is this one 19 year old prettygirl on the motorway, riding a bicycle and not a car, and there are no other cars or trucks on either carriageway accompanying her. She actually finds it all quite therapeutic in a perverse type of way – knowing that she's the only person here. *Maybe the Crash will result in good things. Maybe people will be less selfish after changes are forced into being. Perhaps the Crash will help the climate; with all these factories shut, the traffic jams gone. Even if it delays humanity's demise by a little while.*

Ruby-Rose reaches a crossroad point. There's a big green sign with white stripes and letters, the map telling her that there's a turnpike to the north. From her knowledge that route should lead her across the city border. Yonder she cycles. The roads rise and rise up a winding hillside and it's tough on her calves. When she reaches the top it seems like destiny and she spots the turnstiles of the turnpike in the distance and she feels she deserves a breather and she drinks some water. Then cycles up to the turnstiles and there's nobody about (as she expected) and it looks as if all of them have been broken through during the riots/evacuation – their barriers are bashed up. And she cycles through the mess and suddenly she's on this new bridge with a new blast of air on her frame. Wild, heavenly. ... The turnpike overlooks the motorway network underneath. Massive roads but miniscule from this height and she didn't realise she'd come up so high an altitude. Ruby pauses by the railings and she looks down and the sight of the drop amazes her and the wind holds her eardrums ransom and the purple clouds blotch in the sky. Back on her bike. Wind meddling with the tyres. ... Completes the bridge and comes on to the expanse of the turnpike, in an impressive daunting straight right before her in the land ... except it's not so bad because it's all downhill. Simple riding. Several miles of it, from what she can view, this hard arterial motorway. She kicks on. And the initial descent soon needs to pedalling. She coasts. Then finds that's she's underestimated the steepness of the hill because she's going too fast and she presses her brakes ... (And this memory of Emma returns again. She used to go cycling trips with her in the hills back home. And Emma would , whenever they were atop a summit like this, whizz down the steep road, gleefully as a kid in a swimming pool flume, and never use her brakes. She would just pump it out. Whereas Ruby was too chicken to mimic that. And it'd take her ages to get to the bottom of the hill and Emma would rip her for it.)

Patches of woodland arrive by the roadway. And they bring the leaves. Mushy leaves to the sides and whispery characters in the centre ... and then as she's gotten further along the woods turn to full forest and she watches the shapes of the trees and the whole scene is postcard worthy with colour and she believes *I might just make it now. Despite my crime, I might live on. ...* The downhill bits continue and she succeeds them and she comes to this bizarrely placed bus terminal off the motorway. It's strangely built, as if it were built fifty years back but is still in use. It has a shelter. And Ruby looks up at the clouds. *I could make a stop here and eat something and pause for a moment ... But what if I don't find any shelter further down the road? I'd like to get beyond that border if I can. Before the rainstorm explodes. Have to get past that boundary. I'm not that hungry – I can do it. Looks like the rain will come in the evening. There must be further bus terminals down the line.* And thus, she cycles on. The foliage has this archaic welcoming smell. Her wheels snip and snap the ones that aren't wet. ... The route changes somewhat. Not so straight. Begins to bend through the forest. Hours of cycling, surely. Until she has to stop because she's overdoing it. It's late afternoon now verging on early evening. She doesn't feel it prudent to eat something, for some reason, but she drinks some water and then continues and all that's in front of her is this giant highway and she begins, as it gets darker and darker, to fear that it will rain. That's exactly what happens. ... It starts with an almost merry shower, as if it were Spring. As if the clouds were just pretending to be intimidating all this while. At the same time Ruby-Rose puts her hood up and pretends that this isn't the start. The sky turns into sepia, the road unto yellow-ochre, and it's as if the rain and the new tinges change the hues of her clothes as well, her skin, as if she were in a sepia film now, cycling along, a terrific unwitting actress.

Ruby turns around a new curve in the road and spots this new shape on the road ahead of her. This definitely makes her stop because it's too big to ignore. It's a lorry. Lying in the middle of the route, on its side. And as much as Ruby's tense and keen to get on, the sight is so peculiar that she watches it from afar, wondering what's happened to it. With the rain pinging down on her all around. It's a typical corporate lorry for transporting goods. But it's totally keeled over on its side. What on earth struck it, or made it do that? Ruby goes closer to it. And as she does she sees that the back of the lorry is open. Its doors. And in the hollow gap she can't see anything inside. *So it must've been robbed or held up or something like that? But I don't get why the whole lorry could be toppled over like this.* And then she goes on and gets to the front of the lorry and there's a crunchy indent in the corner of the passenger side, which hangs in the air ... As in, the lorry's front corner is all dented. So it will have been a collision. But why would another vehicle have been coming this side of the road? If that were the case. It's all confusing, mysterious.

Whatever the story is, she cannot stall and examine it.

Powers the pedals and leaves the lorry.

Almost simultaneously the rainclouds buckle above her. They just outrage. Frothing sepia. That tinge is dominated by the sheer range and volume of the water. … Her jeans get sodden. Socks under her boots and her hood doesn't do much to preserve her hair. Deluge. There is no other option aside from cycling and hoping for another shelter. … It's quite sublime. Being doused by all this rain. This vacuum of physical pressure, not cold, or hot, rather dominant and celestial, perfect. Ruby-Rose is nothing versus this mighty power. Nothing around her is. … Nor is it sepia anymore. The shades have befriended the night time. … The streetlamps down the motorway glow in teary dribbles. That's just about all she can see, aside from the lines on the cement, and not even those, because the rainfall's beginning to flood her pathway. And it's tiring on the pedals because she has to push extra hard. … There comes a new corner on the road. And a new hill before it, the levels no longer as kind. And she doesn't think she can take much more physical effort … but she drives up and up and her leg muscles burn. And she gets to the top. And she stops there for a moment. Looking out across her novel. *This deluge is spectacular* she thinks. *I'll be able to bypass through it. I'll find something to give me a bit of shelter. Will get it done.*

Ruby-Rose embarks.

And in not too long she notices this new shape in the distance. This hunky mass of black in the far range, which obviously isn't further forest. A petrol station? She gets hopeful. Now she thinks of it, she's barely seen any urban/human structure for ages. As long as this building or station, whatever it is, has a roof, then she's fine with sheltering under it. The storm's beaten her. She needs cover. … And she gets hasty in her pedalling, Intent on reaching this building. … … … *I have to get there. Have to get there fast. Can't stand this mayhem rain.* And she concentrates on driving as fast as she can and she's looking up at the building rather than down at the cement before her.

And there is this random object lying on the road. She does not see it. It's just a lame item lain on the route.

A scrunched up beer can. It's as stupid and meaningless as that. Some idiot young man threw it into the roadside ditch two weeks back. And the windpower must've lifted it by chance back up onto the road … and Ruby has no notion of it.

And her front tyre skids into it. And her bike jolts forward.

Amok with surprise.

The bike launches sideways. She loses grip of the handlebars and is launched off the saddle. And she lands on her back, and the rear of her skull smacks the concrete. All of it in comic absurdity. … Her mind vanishes. She lies on the floor. Faced up, mouth and eyes cut out. With the bike just next to her. And the rain pounds and pounds and pounds down on both of them.

MARVIN

Day Three in this stranger's house.

Elisa's story about her mother upsets Marvin a great deal. He thinks about it cyclically ever since he told it to her, throughout the night, and it keeps him up, whilst she manages to sleep a little. He does eventually get to sleep himself and he wakes up late morning. Seems like a whole history has passed already in this household, this demented situation. With the two actors. Elisa is still and her eyelids clamped and he doesn't want to bother her. Marvin goes outside into the back garden again, climbing through the kitchen window. He sits on the grass. The change in the oxygen has an overpowering quality as if it is hard to inhale. The vividness of daylight. He watches the fir trees the far end of the garden. Amazing emerald. The evergreen is peaceful, alluring; Marvin gets up and goes closer to them. He stands under the branches and looks up. And he notices this small round shape, tucked into a cleft in the timber, up one of the trunks. *What's that?* Out of curiosity he puts a boot on the lower trunk and lifts himself up by the nearest branch to see closer. (Nice childish joy; climbing a tree.) It's a nest. Bird's nest. This wonderfully small intricate thing about the size of the span of his outstretched hand, as he picks it up. It's woven together with twigs and moss, with such skill, a swirly galaxy, beautiful. Marvin brings it down from the tree. *Do birds return to their nests after the winter? There are no egg shell remnants inside the dome. Surely they just leave it forever when the chicks are hatched and the spring is over. ... So I can take it. I'd like to show Elisa.* Marvin brings it back through the window and he goes into the living room. Elisa stirs, just a little. He still doesn't have the heart to wake her. So he leaves the bird's nest on the coffeetable. ... But then she rouses voluntarily shortly afterwards as he's sitting on the other couch. "Hi," she croaks, when she sees him, and she reaches across to the table for the glass of water. She drinks. Then sees the bird's nest. And she smiles and her eyebrows lift. "What's that?" she says. Marvin picks it up and gives it to her. "I found it in one of the fir trees in the garden. It's incredible isn't it?" – "Yes, it is. ... I wonder how the birds can even do all this work. I couldn't make this, and I'm a human." – "Haha. Yeah I agree." ... She puts the nest back down on the table and thanks him for showing it to her. Marvin asks her if she would like something to eat? He has this tin of semolina pudding in his bag. She says yes please. He wishes he could heat it up for her but he opens it and brings it to her with a spoon. … Elisa is slow and drowsy, she can barely concentrate on lifting the food into her mouth, barely keep her head upright. She manages a few spoonfuls with great effort. "It's really good," she says, "but I can't eat much more right now." Marvin says that's all fine. She says she'd like to retire again. He says that this is also fine: he'll be in the garden if she needs anything. Just call his name and he'll come.

ELISA

She's in a horrible dream and bursts out of it with a glitch in her throat, which sets off this coughing fit. Marvin isn't in the room. Her whole ribcage wracks and heaves and she holds wads of tissue to her mouth and it's quite like suffocating or something near it. And it seems like it'll never stop. ... Then she feels a pop somewhere in her throat. And this spasm of liquid comes out and this new flavour enters her mouth and she spits it out into the tissue. Blood. ... When she sees it, something changes in Elisa. It's not that she *gives up*. It's that she *accepts* a concept. Of course she's sad, spent, broken. *I don't want Marvin to see this blood though.* And so she puts the tissue in her trouser pocket. She lies there for some time. This virus in control of her body; her mind and immune system too weak to tackle it. She hasn't the hardiness for it. *What's the point in even drinking more water?* Elisa wishes that there could be a spell that she could say that would reinvigorate her body; a witchy rhyme or a ritual or sacrifice, which could allow her a few more years. Even if it weren't a long life. Just a little more time in the world – despite how ghastly it is, despite how cruel people are. ... *But not all of them are cruel. Marvin is not.* Elisa reaches for her diary (which is on the coffeetable, very close to that bird's nest). And she writes those two thoughts down inside it. And keeps writing from there, and this is what the rest says: *No, not all people are cruel. Marvin is a great man and I hope he will be remembered. ... I have a feeling that this will be my last diary entry. I hope that, if there's an afterlife, I get to see my mother again. ... Just last night I promised Marvin that I would not leave and I know now that I'm going to fail this promise. ... It's hard not to lose hope in people. Especially since so much of what's happened. After the Crash. Because of the Crash. All of it was because of people. 'Other' people. But I can still hope. That Marvin will go on and influence others. I'll miss him, even if there is no afterlife. I hope that he misses me too. And that he's not angry with me after I go. Bye bye. Elisa.*

ANTHONY BURTON

Just before the storm cascades there is this odd beige colour all across the land.

When the rain comes Anthony picks his pace up. It makes him antsy. The motorway is smooth driving but the clouds just cackle out and spare nothing and the trees by the roadsides all thrash up, the dry leaves on the road get demolished. He keeps his eyes on the road. Tries to gear through the lanes as cleanly as possible, whilst the rain rattles the canopy of his van *spack spack spackle*. The water sloshes down the gutters and it pinneedles the concrete and it keeps coming and coming, relentless. *I was naïve in assuming that I was nearly out of the city. There's some complication to get through yet.* … And it starts to get dark. Anthony switches the floodlights on. Sending the raindashes into silver myriad artwork. … And luckily he's turned his lights on in time. Because he sees this bulky shape up the road. He slows his pace. *What on earth is that?* … This dark cuboid slab on the road. He drives up to it and realises that it's a lorry. Upended and lying on its waist. *What the hell happened here?* It's been gutted. Must've been the looters. But it's just planted there randomly. As if it'd just been punched in the jaw by a giant. Anthony can't guess what went down. He squeezes his van around the far end of the lorry. And looks in the front lorry windows, fearful that there might be a driver in there. But he sees nothing. And he flumes on.

The road gets coily, twisting and turning. Through the pandemonium he rides.

Anthony notices this new urban outline on the horizon. A petrol station perhaps? Maybe he can cut in there and pause for a while.

He's looking up at the station. And then in his lower vision these obstacles pop out. In front of the van.

All of it occurs in milliseconds.

These two shapes appear right before the van amid the rushing rain and he can't recognise what they are. *I can't hit them* and so he swerves to the side to avoid them. … Anthony veers to the centre of the road and he halts just before the barrier. Breathes. He switches his van engine off. … He doesn't currently have his coat on. So he puts it on. And puts his hood up. And steps out of the van and slaps the door shut and his boots plunge into this healthy stream running under him. … He comes around the other side of the van and beholds these shapes on the floor.

One is a bicycle.

The other is a person.

It's a woman. A young woman … Anthony dashes down to her. She's unconscious. Soaked. He lifts her head up. Calls out, can you hear me, can you hear me? (He notices that her face is remarkably beautiful. Alongside her entire physique: she's very pretty.) She's not stirring. Anthony picks her up by the shoulders (which is a bit awkward because she's still wearing her backpack, and it bumps into his groin as he moves) and he drags her across to the van. Her boots make these slicing knifing sounds as they're dragged along. He gets into the driver door and pulls her up after him. Shuts the door. And then he switches on the headlight. And looks at her. She's still alive. Anthony feels the segment under her wrist and there is a pulse there, this dot dot dot of bloodstream. *But how long has she been out in the rain and the cold? How long has she been unconscious?* … He takes off her bag and puts in the back of the van. Anthony has towels in the back too and he retrieves some of them. The woman slumps against the chair, in front of the steering wheel. Anthony feels like it's not his place to be touching a strange woman, in his van. But her sodden hair will only make her colder and so he dries it with the towels. Then he speaks to her and taps her cheeks, trying to get her to wake up. Because he doesn't know what else to do.

RUBY-ROSE

She opens her mouth and takes in this enormous haul of air. Her big eyelashes flicker. Her whole skull stings with pain and there's a new light which is hard not to wince at. She notices pipesmoke. Ruby-Rose knows the smell because her Dad used to smoke a pipe back home. The rain is still there too – in audio – but the noise is different. It clangs and sparks, tinny noises instead of pounding. And wherever she is, is dry. Her brain's still linking the bits together. And then she braces the light and manages to pull her eyes open. First thing she properly sees is a steering wheel and gears and tabs and whatnot ... and she's utterly perplexed *because I don't even know how to drive*. And then she looks across to the left of her and there's this man sitting two seats away, looking at her. He has a blaring white beard and jetblack eyebrows. She screams. And she grabs the door handle next to her and opens it and jumps out. This is her reaction. Jumps into the rain again and the noise resumes its mayhem. But then the man calls to her and he says, "It's all right. I'm no threat! You fell. You fell off your bike. And I found you on the road." ... Ruby-Rose sways. She holds onto the door handle for support. And the rain's making quick work of her body all over again. Feels like she might collapse, that her kneecaps might snap in half. ... "You were unconscious on the road," the man continues. His face is quite calm and tone steady and affirmative. "I'm not trying to abduct you or anything. You can go if you want. Only ... you're probably concussed, so you can stay in the van if you wish. Until the rain stops. It's up to you." He waits for her answer. Her brain tries to formulate a question. Which comes out as, "Where is my bag?" – "Oh," the man replies, "It's here," and he lifts it out from the back and shows it to her and puts it on the driver's seat. "You can go if you want. But I wouldn't keep cycling in this storm if I were you, after you got knocked out. So the offer of temporary shelter is here." ... A rain droplet dribbles down her neck and chest and into her bra. Slides down her breast and catches her nipple. *Yes, I should trust this man. Don't know who he is. But I can trust him, it seems.* "Okay," she says, "thank you, sir." And she gets back up into the van and sits in the seat and she feels like she might vomit and is trying desperately hard not to. They stay there in the front of the van. Bemused. Estranged. The man is socially awkward, wondering whether he's supposed to make conversation and doesn't know where to start. Ruby-Rose should be more grateful and try and say something herself. She has zero strength to do so. ... But then a sudden thought panics her.

"Wait, Mister," she says, turning to him, "what about my bicycle? Is my bike still outside?"

"Your bike is in the back of the van. I put it in the back. If you turn around and look. It was a tight squeeze but I got it in."

Indeed, when she checks, her bike is there. It's dripping. But doesn't look too bashed up.

"There are towels here too," him handing them across to her, "since you've gotten wet again." She thanks him and takes them and scrubs at her hair. (It's hard for Anthony not to watch her dry her hair. It's that luscious a sight. The sheer beauty of her hair. But he manages to look away.) Ruby-Rose looks up at his windscreen which has this berserk spiderweb smash in it. It's dubious and speculative and makes her wonder. But after everything, it is hard to be surprised by such things anymore.

"I'm Anthony Burton," the man says, "by the way."

"I'm Ruby-Rose."

"Hmm. Nice name."

He wasn't going to offer a handshake. But then she offers one. Her fingers are icy. His, hot.

"Never seen rain like this in my 62 years," he says.

"Nor me in my life either."

And they sit together in the dry, damaged, clanging van.

MARVIN

Marvin bows down to her couch with a new glass of water. It's the late night of day four. And all across the morning afternoon and evening Elisa has hardly moved. Aside from when she murmured a jumble of words he couldn't make out. It's nearly midnight now. Her head is in the corner of the couch. And he watches her back. The petite shoulder blades. To check if they're moving. *They're moving a little bit, aren't they?* Marvin hesitates. He's afraid to go closer to her. "Elisa?" he says. No response. So he says her name a bit louder. "Elisa!" Then he touches her shoulder, a bit gruffly, roughly, and her body twitches, so then he says, "Sorry … … Elisa. Wake up for me?" She's still. He puts his palm on her forehead and it's a bit damp. But it's cool, this time. He lifts her onto her front. Her face is blank. Marvin speaks to her. "I thought we made a pact, Elisa," he goes, "I thought we were a great duo. That we would go on." And he jabs his hand under her chin and feels for the jugular beside the windpipe and prays that there will be a bump. *Please don't die on me Elisa please don't die. You can't die after all of this.*

There is no bump, or tremor, only brittle flesh, slowly getting colder. … Marvin pulls the covers up over her face because he can't bear to look at it any longer.

Nor can he stand being in this room. So he leaves it and goes into the kitchen, and the kitchen is too claustrophobic as well, so he opens the window and he climbs outside into the garden, unto a windy night. … There are stars. Between the zooming clouds. Little miracle pinpoints shining. Far, far older vessels than Marvin and Elisa; and they'll live far longer too. Marvin lumbers through the garden, not quite knowing where he's going. And he collapses somewhere on the path and falls into a flowerbed, and the wispy stocks of the spent flowers flutter about his body, as he lies. And cries. He sobs, blubbers, wails out, unleashes all this full grief … for this little girl that has just died, that he should have saved. A person that he failed. The tears run into his lips and he tastes the salt and he weeps until his eyes and his own vocal cords won't work. … *And I'm just a silent wreck in this garden. Not a protagonist. A hero. I could have done far more to save that girl if I'd been less selfish.* … Marvin's wearing his classic coat. And he feels the lumpy object against his left ribcage. From his inside pocket. The handgun.

And he suddenly finds himself pulling it out. He regards this weapon. Then he lifts it to his temple. Points it at his head. *Because what's the point in going on? If you think of it … Why not just end it, right here? One bullet and that will be it? And then there will be no more grief.* He hesitates. And the stars are still there. This is the perfect chance for suicide. But he procrastinates … and then the opportunity flees. Marvin puts the gun back in his pocket and zips it up. Then lies back down again in the perished flowers and looks up at the stars. He does not deserve to look at them; for they are so timelessly beautiful: and so he shuts his eyes.

THE END
A Trade of Grace
Harrison Abbott
27th Sep – 20th Oct 2021.

Printed in Great Britain
by Amazon